EGGS
and Other Stories

JJ TONER

Copyright © 2011 JJ TONER Publishing

EPUB ISBN: 9781908519443

PAPERBACK ISBN: 9781908519474

HARDCOVER ISBN: 9781908519481

Contents

INTRODUCTION TO THE THIRD EDITION

THESE STORIES REPRESENT MY SF output over the past 15 years. None of these stories could be classed "hardcore" or "classical" Science Fiction. A more accurate classification might be "satirical", or – dare I say it – fun SF. For me, this is what Science Fiction should be.

I enjoy the heavy SF hitters as much as the next guy, and I'd walk a country mile to watch a high-budget SF movie. But what I enjoy most is the throwaway remark, the surprising little moments that result from the context or setting of the story.

I owe an enormous debt of gratitude to three giants of Science Fiction. The first is Raphael Aloysius Lafferty who, through his writing, transfused me with his sense of fun. R.A. Lafferty demonstrated, again and again, how rich a source of humor the field of Science Fiction can be. For me, his greatest story was one of his simplest. I read it years ago in an anthology, where I believe it was called *The Disappearer*. I found it again recently in his book *Nine Hundred Grandmothers*. Ace, 1970, where it is called *Seven-Day Terror*. If you like your SF with a twist of fun, find this story and read it.

The second is Robert Sheckley. His short stories are wonderful, and his novel Dimension of Miracles is a truly amazing work of imagination and fun.

Douglas Adams is the third of my heroes. His *Hitchhiker's Guide to the Galaxy* is the ultimate example of fun-SF, full of whimsy, satire, and insightful social commentary.

In this third edition, I have changed the title and the cover. Enjoy the stories. I am planning a major incursion into the field of science fiction with the launch of a new series of novels. Watch out for my Android Wars series in late 2018, early 2019.

Greystones, September, 2021

ALL CREATURES

Pastor Melitus shivers. Not from the cold. The harvest festival is almost upon him, although there is nothing seasonal about the weather. With its thin atmosphere and its distance from the sun, the planet's surface is a deadly 40 degrees below – cold enough to freeze reptilian blood, and far too cold to harvest anything but rare minerals. There are no seasons on Alassak, the occasional snowstorm all that passes for weather. Inside the dome the ambient temperature is a steady 25 degrees, the humidity, as always, a comfortable 15%.

This Godforsaken colony is his third mission. His most recent one was on a lunar outpost in the B-System, and before that he spent two standard Galactic years among the prisoners on Luciflex. That was his most difficult posting, but this mission is a close second. The roughnecks are beyond salvation, and the androids are a godless lot.

As for the indigenous life form – the Quiffos – Pastor Melitus has long since given up trying to communicate with them. The previous incumbent, Pastor Jakob, claimed some successes, but, for Pastor Melitus, carrying the Word of God to the aliens has proved a thankless task. He has had to accept failure. The highest form of life native to the planet, the grotesque, nine-limbed Quiffos are considered intelligent, although their grunting, wheezing, burbling efforts at speech more resemble the bubbling lungs of an old man dying, than any human language.

He slips on his cassock and leaves the sacristy. It's a poor excuse for a chapel with pew spaces for a congregation of no more than 50. Not that that's likely to be a problem. Pierrepoint, the planet Governor, may attend the service with his wife, and he has promised to rustle up a few of his juniors. The rest are less certain: some military personnel, perhaps, and there are three freighter transports in the dock. He might get one or two from each ship, if he's lucky.

It is difficult not to surrender to despair. The pastor has to continually remind himself that the Almighty won't object to the size of the church nor the numbers in his congregation.

With a slight tremor in his hands, he throws open the doors and steps outside. He checks his watch. The sun is high in the sky, bathing everything in an even, soft light, filtered by the envelope of the massive dome.

He casts his gaze about. Towering above the chapel to his left stands the administration block, a kaleidoscope of glass, and to his right the massive, brooding bulk of the military barracks. Something resembling a tumbleweed blows across the deserted path leading to the church. He checks his watch again. Five standard minutes to go.

What if no one turns up? Another riot among the dome constructor crews, or another of the fatal accidents, could stop the Governor and his staff from attending. Could this be the first harvest festival ever to score a duck anywhere in the Six Systems of the galaxy? And if that happened, surely his whole mission would be deemed a failure. He might be sent back to Luciflex to minister to the enslaved miners for the rest of his days. A ring of icy sweat breaks out under his collar.

He scurries back inside and drops to his knees on a pew. "Dear Lord, I know I have tried your patience in the past, praying for an easier posting, and I know my faith has wavered from time to time, but I have devoted my life to the ministry. You know the sacrifices that I've made in your name. Dear Lord, please grant me a congregation this day. Don't make me bear the shame of an empty chapel on the day of your harvest festival."

He hears a noise behind him and turns. Filling the doorway stands a figure in silhouette, its nine boneless limbs writhing about its body.

The alien lurches forward, and the pastor runs to the sanctuary of his pulpit. Moving with disconcerting speed and agility, the Quiffo approaches the altar. It is carrying a loose brown bundle with something squirming inside. It places the bundle before the altar and takes a place in the front pew, supporting its hideous head on two of its appendages. It is followed by another Quiffo, and another. A total of six Quiffos enter. Each drops a squirming bundle before the altar and perches beside its companions on the front pew.

Pastor Melitus raises his eyes to Heaven and prays a silent 'thank you' to the Lord. "Welcome, friends," he says. "If you'll all stand we will start with a hymn."

The Quiffos shuffle about, rearranging their limbs. The pastor starts the tape recorder and the chapel fills with organ music. He begins to sing and the Quiffos are inspired to join in, filling the chapel with a cacophony of sounds the like of which has never before been heard in any Christian chapel anywhere in the Six Systems of the Galaxy.

"All things bright and beautiful..."

EGGS

Feeling irritable and bloated, Professor Karl Brown sat hunched at his desk in his shorts and shirtsleeves. The air conditioning unit groaned and rattled above the window behind him. The temperature gauge on the wall was steady at 108 degrees Fahrenheit. The temperature outside was ten degrees higher.

"This hellish heat makes me irritable and bloated," he said.

Lissa, his secretary, looked up from her keyboard. "How *is* Mrs. Brown?" she said in her husky voice. Lissa's voile smock clung to her upper body. She was aware that the professor was getting an eyeful, but she was past caring; she could feel her brain simmering gently in the afternoon heat.

"Irascible," he replied, "and acting weird."

A plump bluebottle meandered drunkenly across the room before diving headlong into the *Zappomatic.* The machine fizzled and the fly was gone.

"Weird how?"

"She's building a nest in the garage," he said, wiping the sweat from his eyebrows.

"That is a little unusual," Lissa said.

"It's made out of cardboard boxes, padded with news-papers, blankets, and cushions."

"How big is it?"

"About twelve feet in diameter, and yea tall." He indicated a height of about four feet.

Lissa's nervous laugh was interrupted by a cough.

The professor continued, "When I left for work this morning, Marona was preparing to spray-paint the whole contraption. She was dressed in overalls and a face-mask."

"What color?"

"Blue."

"Blue paint?"

"Blue overalls. The paint was lime green."

"Now, that is strange." Lissa coughed again.

The telephone rang. Lissa picked it up.

"Karl?" rasped the voice at the other end of the line.

"Just one moment," Lissa said sweetly. "Putting you through."

"Who is it?"

Lissa raised an eyebrow and flicked the call-transfer button.

"Hello Marona..." The professor squirmed in his seat. "Yes, dear... Fine... What? Fine...What? Fine...How much?... One liter. Okay... Five thirty... Yes, dear... Fine... Yes, dear... Of course... And a Hershey bar... *Two* Hershey bars... Right... No, I won't forget."

He put the telephone down again. "That was my wife," he said.

***

"Honey, I'm home."

There was no answer.

He called up the stairs, "Sweetpie?" No answer.

The professor went into the garage. His wife's nest was empty. It was grotesque, five feet high in the center, filling the back end of the garage. Its shape suggested a crouching giant with a hunchback. He could see where she had run out of paint.

He found her locked in the bathroom upstairs.

"I have your paint, Sweetness," he said through the locked door. When there was no answer he added, "Are you all right in there, Sugar?"

"No," she shouted back. "I'm not."

"What's the matter, Sweetie?"

"It's the baby," she cried.

"What is?"

"It's arrived,"

"That's impossible, Sweetpie. It's too early," he replied, rather stupidly.

"Look in the bedroom."

The professor pushed open the bedroom door with trepidation and closed eyes. His mind was busy with the math. She was still in her second trimester, maybe twenty-six weeks. If she had given birth this early – he shuddered, then counted to three and opened his eyes.

The egg lay on the middle of the bed. It was blue. It was about the size of a full-grown porpoise, bigger than a tuna, certainly, but smaller than a dolphin. It was undeniably blue, and yet there was something fiercely purple and milky white about its blueness – and with a hint of scarlet mixed in. Gingerly, he reached out and poked it with a finger. It felt soft, like rubber, slightly tacky, and eerily warm.

Tiny blood vessels were visible just beneath the surface. It was fairly opaque, although some of the light from the window seemed to be passing through it, making it glow duskily. Looking straight at it, the professor couldn't see beyond the surface, but looking away he thought he could make out a dark smudge – a shape, perhaps – deep inside.

Then the shape inside moved, the skin of the egg rippled like molasses, and the professor leapt six inches off the ground.

He closed the bedroom door and returned to the bathroom.

"What have you done?" he shouted at the closed door.

"Nothing. I've done nothing."

"What is that on the bed?"

"I don't know. It just...popped out."

"What were you doing?" he said.

"I was trying on a hat."

He considered the implications of this statement, but could find none.

"Karl?"

"Yes, Sweetie, I'm still here."

"What is that... thing? On the bed."

"It looks like an egg."

"I know what it looks like, but what is it?"

"It's an egg, Sweetpie."

"But it's blue," she wailed.

"It's a blue egg," he said.

"And what about my baby?"

"I think the baby's inside."

"It's dead, isn't it?" She sniffled.

"No, I don't think so. I think it's alive."

"How can it be alive?"

"I don't know, but I saw it move."

She opened the bathroom door and went into the bedroom. He waited outside, like an expectant father. Then she fetched three blankets from the linen cupboard.

"We need to keep it warm," she said. "Put the heating on."

The temperature gauge on the wall was steady at 109 degrees. Outside, it was still ten degrees higher.

She sniffed. "Help me lift him downstairs." He caught the dubious pronoun, but let it slide. They carried the egg down to the garage, and lifted it into Marona's nest. She arranged the cushions and blankets around it carefully. Then she climbed in and lowered herself onto the egg.

"Go fetch the duvet," she said.

"You don't have to sit on it."

"Why not?"

"It's not necessary. It's," he checked the thermometer on the wall, "a hundred and twelve in here." There was no air conditioning in the garage.

"Oh, so now you're an expert," she snorted. "Where's my Hershey bars?"

***

Marona spent the night in the garage. In the morning, her legs were stiff, her joints ached, and she couldn't straighten her back. She hobbled into the kitchen.

"What's the matter with you?" the professor asked through a mouthful of muesli.

"I'm stiff all over."

He smiled smugly; he had spent a comfortable night alone in bed.

"It's not natural," he said.

"What's not natural?"

"Sitting on it all night."

"Oh, and laying the thing in the first place, that was natural, was it?"

"It could be an evolutionary throwback," he said thoughtfully.

"What does that mean?"

"Well, like the way some birds became flightless, and whales returned to the sea."

"You're making no sense, Karl," she snapped. "When did whales leave the sea?"

"Whales are mammals descended from land animals like the hippopotamus."

"And?"

"All land mammals evolved from sea creatures originally, so whales went full circle. They evolved from the sea to the land, and then reverted back to the sea."

"So I'm a whale? Is that what you're saying?"

"No, of course not. Like all placental mammals, whales give birth to live young."

"So what am I?"

He gave that some thought before answering thoughtlessly, "Insects lay eggs."

"I'm a bug!" she wailed.

"And spiders," he added, rather recklessly.

"Are you saying I'm a spider?" she shrieked.

"No of course not. Birds lay eggs, but you're clearly not a bird."

"So what am I?"

"Reptiles lay eggs," he said, foolishly.

She began to cry.

***

He called Dr. Wayne McPayne, the family doctor, and made an appointment.

"An egg, you say?" The expression on the doctor's face defied description.

"Yes, Doctor, a blue egg."

"And she's building a nest, you say?"

"In the garage. Yes."

The doctor's strange expression darkened. "Have you been drinking?" he said.

"Hasn't everyone, in this heat?"

"How much?"

"I don't know. A few beers now and then. Why?"

"You don't look drunk. Did anything unusual happen last week?"

"Like what?"

"I don't know. Anything out of the ordinary. Hot flashes, perhaps."

"I had a slight head cold on Tuesday."

"Did anything out of the ordinary happen to your wife?"

"She drank half a glass of wine on Monday. Perhaps that had something to do with it."

The doctor shook his head. "Half a bottle, maybe, but half a glass shouldn't have had that effect."

"What should we do, Doctor?"

"Bring her in to see me, and bring the—bring *it* with you."

"I can't."

"Why not?"

"She's brooding."

The doctors' eyebrows did a highland jig. "You mean...?"

Brown nodded. "She just sits there all day and all night."

"Well that's certainly an overreaction. Tell her from me, if she wraps it up and keeps it nice and warm, it should be fine."

"You think it might hatch?"

"I really have no idea."

The next day, he had a follow-up call from Dr McPayne.

"I've spoken with the health authorities. They've put together a small team to look into your... problem. Could they meet you in your office this afternoon?"

The team consisted of a psychiatrist, a psychologist and a lawyer. The university sent along a man from human resources, as an observer.

After the introductions, the psychologist asked, "How long have you been having these schizoid delusions?"

"Gross reality distortions," the psychiatrist corrected him.

"Fanciful imaginings," the human resources man said.

"I beg your pardon," Professor Brown replied. "They are not schizoid imaginings, nor are they fanciful distortions of reality."

"I thought so," said the lawyer. "Hallucinatory manifestations."

"No, not those either," Brown said. "My wife has laid an egg."

The psychologist glanced at the psychiatrist. The psychiatrist shook his head sadly and clicked his tongue.

"I advise you to say nothing further," the lawyer said.

The human resources man asked the professor if he would like to take some time off work.

That evening, Professor Brown came across a small article on the science page of his newspaper. His heart was in his mouth as he read it. Field biologists had discovered a small shrew in Malaysia that had switched from placental to oviparous reproduction. Environmentalists had seized on this remarkable discovery and were using it to demonstrate the effects of global warming. One famous evolutionist of the Dawkins School discounted the whole story. She was quoted as saying that "an evolutionary change of this magnitude, while not inconceivable, would take several million years."

The professor explained the problem to Dr. Velikof Zonk III, in the university's zoology department. Brown took Zonk home and showed him the egg. Zonk examined it and took several photographs, before Marona sent both men packing.

They returned to Dr. Zonk's office.

"Under normal circumstances..." Dr Zonk began, peering into the bowl of his pipe, probing and tamping the contents with a strange tool. When the pipe was belching smoke, he clamped his teeth around the stem. "Where vas I?"

"Under normal circumstances?"

"Ah yes. Under normal circumstances one would not eggspect such an occurrence. I believe I am right in saying that on ootocoid human is quite rare. Indeed, such an event may very well be unique in the history of ah..."

"Humanity?"

"Evolution. But that is not to say that such a thing has never happened before."

"You mean it may have?"

"It is conceivable that an eggceptional event of this sort has occurred but vas never recorded, or that having been recorded, it may haff been..."

"Forgotten?"

"Eggspinged from the written archive."

"Expunged."

"Precisely."

"And from the zoological standpoint, what do you make of it?"

"Speaking as a zoologist, I would haff to say that this sort of development is not entirely uneggspected. I mean, the biosphere has been under sustained attack for more than two millennia now. Ve can only guess at the residual effects of global varmink, coupled with the high levels of atmospheric pollution, not to mention the depletion of the ozone layer. Evolution has never been known to stand still, and environmental disruption on such a global scale must, of necessity, result in evolutionary change of one sort or another."

"So are you saying this is something normal, natural and unremarkable?"

"Hardly any of those, Brown. I would characterize it as an evolutionary reaction to eggstreme environmental stimuli. Unusual, certainly, but not entirely..."

"Unexpected?"

"Unpredictable."

"Was it something we did?"

"Not at all," Zonk said, puffing on his pipe. "Think of it as an evolutionary probe, a tentative adaptation by humankind in its search for new vays to survive in changing and ah... challenging conditions, a striking example of Mother Nature's ability to adapt, and nothing more than a piece of..."

"Bad luck?"

"Mutational opportunism."

"You mean like a magician's trick?"

"If you like."

"A rabbit from a hat?"

"Something similar, *ja*."

"What should we do?" Brown asked.

"Leave it with me," Zonk replied. "The first thing I need to do is to conduct a search of the available literature."

"You'll keep this information under wraps?"

"Naturally. Of course."

"Promise me, Zonk. Not a word of this must get out."

"I promise. You can trust me."

Word quickly spread around the university and then around the town. And as is the way with small towns and the clergy, Father Lafferty, the parish priest, heard all about it. He made an urgent appointment to see the bishop.

"An egg, you say, Father?"

"Yes, your Grace, a large, blue egg."

"And you think the... ah... contents are alive?"

"So it would appear, your Grace."

The bishop levered himself from his chair and strolled to the window. His vestments clung to his legs as he walked, and there was a damp patch spreading from the middle of his back. It was early spring and yet the temperature outside was a raging 110 degrees.

"We're in for another hot summer," he said.

Father Lafferty said nothing. Pronouncements like this from a bishop could not be contradicted; the bishop represented his Holiness the pope, and the pope, as everyone knew, was infallible. Besides, it didn't take a bishop to predict the weather; no one could remember the last cool summer in Maryland, or anywhere else in the United States. As for the old country, it was thirty years since the central bog lands had dried up and turned to desert.

The air conditioning unit on the wall belched and emitted a small plume of steam.

"Do you think it might be viable?" The bishop's tone was sharp. He fixed the priest with a hepatic eye.

"I have no idea, your Grace. We can only wait and watch."

The bishop returned to his desk. Slowly, and with much puffing, he lowered his huge frame into his chair. He took a moment to catch his breath, then he shook his head. "I don't think so, Father," he said. "Bold and decisive action is called for. What we need is a plan."

Father Lafferty's heart sank. He groaned inwardly. It was because of the failure of one of the bishop's earlier plans that the priest had been sent to rot in this dead-end corner of Christianity.

***

It had started in the African jungle many years earlier, of course. The first few times it happened, the tribal shamans deemed it a curse visited on those who had strayed from the tribal way. Those few afflicted were labeled "bird-women" and banished from their families. Some were cast out from their tribes; some may have been put to the sword to assuage the anger of arcane gods.

As it began to happen more and more frequently, tribal shamans were called to cast their spells to save the tribe from this terrible curse. These men, descended from generations of wise men, drank or smoked their hallucinogenic concoctions and entered their vision worlds. Then they called on all their magic, all their cunning, but to no avail. This was something contrary to their understanding of the way of the gods, a truly great curse, undoubtedly the work of the Demon-God N'ghalla, the crocodile, who dwelt in the dark underworld.

***

Professor Brown offered the priest a drink.

"Irish whiskey if you have it," Father Lafferty said. "Just a small drop. It's a bit early, yet." It was nine-thirty in the morning.

The air conditioning unit moaned like a dyspeptic banshee.

"I have Bourbon."

The professor poured a generous measure and handed Father Lafferty the glass. The priest swallowed half of the contents in one gulp.

"Nice room," the priest said.

"I like it," the professor replied.

"Yes, I could get used to a study like this."

"Indeed."

There was a pronounced – one might say a pregnant – pause. Father Lafferty opened his mouth and then closed it again without speaking. He threw back the rest of his whisky.

"Another drop?" the professor asked, and the priest handed him the glass.

As he poured another, less generous drink, the professor said, "I think there's something on your mind, Father."

"You could say that," Father Lafferty replied.

"Is it about that students' charity week prank?" The sophomores had climbed the church facade and put a bra on the statue of the Virgin Mary.

Father Lafferty shook his head. "It's about your wife," he said.

"My wife?"

"The bishop has asked me to talk to you about the, um...situation."

"And what situation would that be?"

Father Lafferty crossed his legs, then uncrossed them again. "It's about your wife's condition."

"My wife is expecting a baby," the professor said. "Is that what you mean?"

"Well yes. I understand that she *was* expecting a baby."

"She still is."

"Yes, but I understand that her condition has changed." Father Lafferty squirmed in his seat like a snail in a salt mine.

"In what way?" The professor crossed his arms firmly across his chest. He had no intention of making things any easier for the cleric.

"I'm told that she has..."

The professor said nothing.

"I know it sounds crazy, but I've heard that she..."

The professor smiled unctuously. He raised an eyebrow.

"The bishop has asked me to explain..."

"What?"

"The Church's position on..."

"On what?"

"On unnatural practices."

"Such as?"

"Such as the condition of your wife."

"What are you trying to say, Father?"

Father Lafferty took a deep breath. "The Church considers your wife's condition a... an abomination—"

"A what?"

"—that must be terminated."

"What are you saying?"

"It's clearly the work of the Devil. God would never have sanctioned such an aberration."

"The work of the Devil, you say?"

"Yes." Father Lafferty finished the second glass of whisky and stood up.

"What are you suggesting, Father?"

"You must get rid of it."

"Say that again, Father. I think I must have misheard you."

"The bishop has asked me to instruct you—"

"You want me to *abort* my wife's baby?" Professor Brown wiped the sweat from his brow.

"It is not a baby. It is an abomination. Killing an abomination is not – what you said."

"ABORTION!" The professor roared, jumping out of his chair.

"I understood you were a good Catholic, Professor."

"Yes, but —"

"As a good Catholic you must obey your bishop."

"Under normal circumstances, maybe, but—"

"And the bishop's order is unequivocal."

The professor strode to the door and held it open. "Not going to happen," he said. "I wish you good day, Father."

***

Professor Zonk's paper appeared in the April edition of *Natural Selection* under the title "*The Ootocoid Woman: An Evolutionary Breakthrough.*" As there was a paucity of news that week, the article was reproduced by the local newspaper. But it was only after some of Zonk's photos appeared on the Internet that *The New York Times* science correspondent gave it the full treatment and the tabloids picked it up. They ran the story on their front pages with headlines like "MOTHER LAYS EGG", "REP-TILE WOMAN" and "HIDEOUS MONSTER: WILL IT HATCH?"

The television companies set up their cameras outside the professor's house, erecting a huge canvas canopy to shield their equipment from the brutal sun. They tried to interview him as he left for work in the morning.

"Is it true, Professor?"

"Do you know why it happened?"

"Can we talk to your wife?"

Professor Brown refused to answer any of their questions.

When he arrived home in the evening they were still there.

"Can we take a picture of it?"

"We'd like to do an interview for the evening news."

The professor brushed them aside. "Leave us alone!" he roared as he slammed the door.

They shouted through his mail slot: "You can't hide forever, Professor!" and "The public has a right to know."

He found Marona in the garage, weeping quietly. The egg was hidden beneath her. Pulling himself up onto the nest, he put his arms around her shoulders. She rested her head on his chest and wailed.

"Why won't they go away? Why won't they leave us alone?"

"There, there, Honey." The professor patted her head. "It's not the end of the world. Here, have a Hershey bar."

***

It soon became clear that Marona's case was not unique. A woman in Australia and two in the Far East were discovered hiding out with blue eggs. A Biology professor in the James Cook University of Townsville published a hastily written paper which hypothesized that placental reproduction in large mammals could be supplanted by the oviparous method under the influence of extreme climate change.

Soon after that, the media coverage turned hostile. For the first time in recorded history all the main churches were united on one theme: this aberration was contrary to God's Law. A device of Science, an Instrument of the Devil, it must be discouraged, outlawed, eradicated. Any woman found in possession of "Satan's Seed" must surrender it to the authorities for destruction.

***

Then one day when Professor Brown returned from work, he found an angry mob at his door bearing firebrands.

"Bring her out!" they shouted, and they threw bricks at the windows.

The mob was too late. Marona had gone. The professor searched for her. She was not in the house or the garage. He searched the house a second time, top to bottom, but she was nowhere to be found. The egg was missing as well. He rang her cell phone and found it in her underwear drawer. He rang Marona's best friend, Pam, but Pam hadn't seen her.

He shouted back at the mob. He told them his wife was gone. They didn't believe him, not until a couple of the ringleaders had barged their way in and searched for themselves. After that, the mob dispersed.

The professor waited until dark before calling the police.

Belldene was far too small a town to warrant its own police station, so it fell under the bailiwick of the station at Tobias, three miles to the south. Even with a following wind, Tobias was not much bigger than two Belldenes added together and its police force consisted of just one trooper (first class) and one smart, black bicycle.

"My name is Professor Brown. I want to report a missing person."

Dermot Fingerwell, Trooper First Class, said, "And who would that be?"

"It's my wife. She's gone missing."

"Name?"

"Marona Brown."

"When did you last see your wife?"

"This morning."

"Perhaps she's gone shopping."

"But she's expecting."

"Perhaps she's gone shopping."

***

Early the next morning, when Trooper Fingerwell arrived at the Browns' house, the TV crews descended on him like a swarm of locusts. Refusing to answer any of their questions, he parked his smart black bicycle on the porch and rang the doorbell.

Professor Brown opened the door and let the Trooper in.

Fingerwell flipped open his notebook and went through the routine questions: Had the missing person made contact? Had the professor checked all her usual haunts? Her friends? Neighbors? Was she depressed, unhappy about anything? Did she have a car of her own? (No) A credit card? (Yes)

They went upstairs to check if any of her clothing had been taken. And that was when the professor first began to realize that his wife had left him. He gave Trooper Fingerwell a recent photo of his wife.

"I wouldn't worry too much," Fingerwell said. "I'll check with the railroad and bus companies. I expect she just needed a break. She'll probably ring in a day or two."

"Right."

"Give us a ring when you hear from her."

"And if I don't?"

"Give it a week. If you still haven't heard from her by then, call me back."

The doorbell rang that evening. Professor Brown ran to the door and flung it open.

"Marona—"

Several microphones and tape recorders were thrust under his nose.

"Where's your wife, sir?"

"Where is she?"

"Do you know where your wife is, Professor?"

The professor reeled back under the deluge of questions.

"My wife has gone away," he said, his voice barely audible.

"What did he say?"

"She's left you, Professor? Is that what you mean?"

"I don't know. She's missing. That's all I can say."

A shrill voice from the back shouted, "What have you done with her, you fiend?"

The professor slammed the door and went back to his armchair.

***

Unrelenting, the intense heat pounded down, shimmering off the pavement. All around her, in the fields and in the trees, Marona could sense Nature busily adjusting to the new reality, like a great engine shifting gears.

She cut a lonely figure at the side of the road, clutching her precious cargo in a small sports bag. She was not un-attractive and it wasn't long before she was picked up by a truck driver hauling supermarket supplies.

"Where you headed, little lady?" the driver said, tilting his hat back on his head and wiping the sweat from his face.

"West," she replied.

He asked her a few sociable questions; she kept her an-swers as vague as possible. She had walked ten miles across open country before venturing onto the freeway. Her first objective was to cross the state line; once she had left her home state, she reckoned her chances of escaping would multiply.

He dropped her at a truck stop where she found another ride. By nightfall, she was in Ohio. She had followed a zigzag path that would make it difficult for anyone trying to follow her. The country was vast and she knew how to disappear. She checked in at a roadside motel, using a made-up name and paying in advance with cash. She knew not to use her credit card.

Lifting the egg carefully from the bag, she placed it on the bed. She sat and watched the blurred shape of her son, illuminated by the bedside lamp, stretching and moving inside his egg. She could see his head, his arms, his legs. She sang to him for hours. At eleven o'clock she wrapped the egg in blankets and a duvet. She slipped out to an all-night convenience store for supplies and fixed herself a light supper of tinned tuna, bagel and fruit, followed by a couple of Hershey bars.

In the morning, early, she hit the road again and by the end of the second day she was in Evansville, Indiana, 600 miles and three states from Belldene, Maryland.

***

A week after his wife's departure, Professor Brown decided it was time to reclaim his garage. He dismantled Marona's ridiculous nest, throwing out any soft furnishings that had been contaminated with lime green paint and filling a plastic bag with Hershey bar wrappers.

Underneath the elaborate structure he discovered a nest of mice. He did his best to catch them, but they proved too elusive, too lively for a man of his age. On his way home that evening he dropped round to the premises of the local pest controller, seeking advice. The young man behind the counter looked familiar.

"Don't I know you?" the professor said.

"Yes, Professor," the man replied. "I used to sell the *Zappomatic.*"

"I remember. I bought one from you."

"I hope it's still working for you. As you can see, I've moved on since those days. I now provide specialized pest control services to the people of Baltimore County."

"I have an infestation of mice in my garage," the professor said. "I wondered what method you would recommend for removing them."

The young man produced a packet of white powder marked POISON.

"This should do the trick," he said. "Use liberal amounts along the foot of the walls. Just make sure no one in your household swallows any of the stuff. It's pretty lethal."

***

It was 10 AM, early siesta time in Baltimore County. In the police station in Tobias, Trooper First Class Dermot Fingerwell had finished the easy crossword and given up on the cryptic one. He loosened his tie, undid a couple of his shirt buttons, tilted his chair back and his hat over his face, lifted his feet onto his desk and closed his eyes.

The door burst open. Fingerwell awoke with a start. He struggled to his feet and reached for his gun. His holster was empty.

Before him stood Baltimore County's Lieutenant Harry Brock. The Lieutenant looked hot the way a demon from the fires of Hell looks hot. His face was bright red, his upper lip covered in sweat and there were large damp patches under his arms.

"Where's your gun, Trooper?" the Lieutenant boomed.

"I've been cleaning it," Trooper Fingerwell answered. "It's around here somewhere."

"Never mind that. Get me something cold to drink. We have work to do."

Brock collapsed into a chair. Fingerwell fetched two beers from the cooler. He handed one of the beers to the Lieutenant and opened the other one for himself.

Fingerwell repeated the dreaded four-letter word. "Work?"

An hour later Lieutenant Brock was gone, leaving Trooper Fingerwell alone again to count the cost. With a huge sigh he carried eight empty beer cans out to the trash.

He hated these flying visits. He hated how he could never fully relax, never knowing when someone from County might come crashing through his door to check up on him. Most of all he hated Lieutenant Harry Brock. He hated the man's ridiculous haircut, his piercing eyes and the crisp creases in his trousers.

He stared at his notepad where the Lieutenant had written the names of three local women who had recently gone missing. Nancy Goodyer, Shelly Tarr and Marona Brown. As all three women were pregnant when they disappeared, all three cases had been elevated to the status of major investigations. County would be sending a team to get these investigations under way in the next day or so. Trooper Fingerwell sighed again and went to his cooler for another beer.

***

Professor Karl Brown sat hunched at his desk in his boxers and vest, a glass of iced tea by his elbow. The air conditioning unit rattled and shook behind him. The temperature gauge on the wall read 111 degrees. The temperature outside was eight or nine degrees higher.

"This abominable heat makes me irritable," he said. "Since my wife left, my underwear seems to itch like crazy."

Lissa looked up from her keyboard. "No word from Mrs. Brown?" she said in her husky voice. Lissa had abandoned her voile smock. She'd taken to wearing her bikini at work; it was the only way she could bear to sit at her desk at all. She was aware that the professor now spent most of the day ogling her, but she was past caring. He was a fine figure of a man, all considered, and if his wife didn't want him, well, he was fair game. Lissa had been alone ever since her last boyfriend, a *Zappomatic* salesman, had dumped her, two years earlier.

"Nothing," he replied. "I think she's gone forever."

"Don't say that, Professor. I'm sure she'll be back some day soon."

He shook his head, peering at her through hooded eyes.

"More iced tea?" she said.

"Yes please."

She stepped across the room carrying the iced tea. She topped up his glass, then placed the jug on his desk and turned her back to him.

"Would you mind?" she said. "My bikini strap feels too tight. Would you mind loosening it for me?"

Minutes later, Lissa was on her back under the professor's desk, watching over his shoulder as a large bumblebee droned purposefully across the room. The bee dove headlong into the *Zappomatic,* the machine fizzled and the insect disappeared. Lissa could feel her brain bubbling gently in the heat.

***

Marona was running out of money. She knew she couldn't find a normal job – not without revealing her social security number – so she resolved to live her life like the illegals all around her. She found casual cleaning work in a small library. It was irritating to be surrounded by staff who knew little or nothing about books. She frequently had to bite her lip when the librarians showed their ignorance, like when one young staff member confused Henry James with O. Henry.

She moved into a boarding house, spinning the landlady a story which was straight out of Catherine Cookson. Driven from the family home in California by a cruel and violent husband, Marona had to lay low and build a new life for herself, ever watchful lest the evil man discover her whereabouts and drag her back to her previous life of terror and torture.

The day the egg hatched was the happiest day of Marona's life. The baby girl that emerged was blonde, big and healthy. Marona named her Pam, after her best friend. The child had a small tooth that fell out after a couple of days and there was something odd about her belly-button. Otherwise, young Pam was a perfect specimen.

"I never even noticed that you were pregnant," Mrs. Windermere, the landlady, said.

"It's my figure," Marona said. "My sister's just the same. She had twelve and never a one ever showed."

"Twelve! Mercy!" Mrs. Windermere cried, exercising a large fan.

***

Lissa and Karl's secret was out within a couple of days and tongues began to wag, the way tongues do in small towns. Word eventually reached the ears of the police special investigation squad in Tobias.

Trooper Fingerwell put in a call to county headquarters. Lieutenant Brock listened to what Fingerwell had to say.

"Hanky panky, you say?" said Brock.

"Yes, sir, and worse, by all accounts."

"You're sure about this, Fingerwell?"

"Yes, sir. No question."

"Right, that's it. Bring him in."

The special investigation unit questioned the professor for days. They tried everything short of actual torture, but he wouldn't crack. They had a missing wife, a large insurance policy – not yet claimed – and a mistress. What they didn't have was a body, so they dug up the professor's garden. They took a jackhammer to his cellar floor. They used cadaver dogs and x-ray technology on every patch of open ground in the university. They found nothing.

Finally, Lieutenant Brock ordered the case handed over to the District Attorney's office, where it was given to a young lawyer called Ambrose Neal. A recent graduate of Harvard, Neal was ambitious and he had read every one of John Grisham's novels. After studying the files of the case he recommended to the District Attorney that they should proceed to prosecute.

"On what charge?" the DA said.

"Murder one!" Neal declared.

"You're sure about this?"

"Positive, sir. I guarantee a guilty verdict."

"Well, if you're certain…"

Neal was far from certain. In fact he knew that, given the evidence to hand, the examining magistrate would throw out the case at the preliminary hearing; it would never go to trial. He was relying on the "Grisham factor." Something unexpected was bound to turn up.

And something did. A few days before the hearing a young pest controller came forward and offered to testify that he had sold a packet of lethal poison to the professor. Ostensibly for the eradication of a mouse infestation, the poison could easily have been used to eradicate the professor's wife.

***

"State your name and occupation," the defense attorney said.

"Dr. Velikof Zonk, professor of zoology."

The lawyer handed him a copy of the April edition of *Natural Selection*. "And you are the author of the article on page thirty-seven, are you not?"

"I am."

"What is the title of the paper?"

" '*The Ootocoid Woman: An Evolutionary Breakthrough.*' "

"Tell the jury, in your own words, please, Professor, what the article is about."

It was touch and go. The science was more than the judge and jury could cope with, but they had all read the newspaper accounts. The judge demanded to know how it was possible that any mammal, let alone a human, could reproduce in this way. Zonk pointed out that there were many egg-laying mammals, like the monotremes of South America and Australia.

When Dr. Zonk produced his photos of the egg, they were convinced. The missing woman had indeed laid a large blue egg! Professor Brown's defense attorney drove home the most salient point.

"Would you say that the changes to Mrs. Brown's body are significant?"

"Beyond question."

"How significant?"

"Eggstremely."

"Would you say that what has happened to Mrs. Brown is significant on an evolutionary scale?"

"I would."

"Please think carefully before you answer my next question, Dr. Zonk."

Zonk nodded.

"Would you say that these changes constitute the emergence of a new species?"

"I would."

"You are sure about that?"

"Absolutely certain."

Further crucial evidence was provided for the defense by the bishop. In testimony peppered with the words "unholy" and "abomination", he confirmed that he had ordered a termination of the pregnancy, as whatever was inside the egg could not have been human.

The newspapers had a field day. ALIEN CREATURES AMONGST US. JUDGE RULES EGG-BABY NOT HUMAN.

The trial collapsed. In the first place, the evidence for foul play was entirely circumstantial, and second, and more importantly, as the victim was a member of a new species, a charge of murder could not stand.

***

"Good morning, Professor," Lissa said.

She had emptied both filing cabinets and placed them on their sides across the corner of the room. The resulting triangular space she'd filled with bundles of papers, files and reports.

"What are you doing?" he asked.

"I'm sorting out these papers," she said, pulling a can of spray paint from her handbag.

The professor was horrified. "Those are my reports, my files, my class notes, my student records. What d'you think you're doing?"

Then it struck him. She was building a nest.

FIRST CONTACT

Cyril Brasenose carried his latte into the Signal Monitor room. He had a couple books to read and he would waste an hour or two on Twookie, but even so he knew the time would drag.

Sixteen miles away in downtown Palo Alto, Professor Bertrand Wheelright finished his ham and eggs with a satisfied sigh. Tossing a bacon rind to Fido, his golden retriever, he rang his bookie and placed a bet: $1,000 on Flatulent Pig in the Kentucky Derby. Then he rose from his chair and headed into the hall, his footsteps dogged by an increasingly excited Fido. Casting a grateful eye on the photograph of Carl Sagan mounted on the wall at the foot of the stairs, the professor mumbled, "Thank you, Carl," as he did every morning. He reached for Fido's leash hanging on a hook behind the door. The retriever's eyes lit up. He barked and did an ecstatic twirl.

At that moment the telephone rang. The professor picked it up and was greeted by a babbling voice, making no sense.

"You're making no sense, man," said the professor. "Stop babbling, take a deep breath and start again. Start by telling me who you are."

"This is Cyril Brasenose, sir, at SETI. We have an incoming signal, and it's definitely intelligent. It's exactly what we've been looking for all these years!"

"You're sure it's not local? You know how atmospheric conditions can deflect land-based radio traffic—"

"I've checked, Professor. The signal is definitely extraterrestrial, origin somewhere in M45, the Pleiades. I have prepared a short press release. Would you like me to read it to you?"

"Don't let's be hasty, Nosebag," said the professor. "Better run the signal through the translation software first. Find out what it says and call me straight back."

The professor hung up. Mrs. Wheelwright stuck her head round the kitchen door. "Still here, Bert?"

"I've had a call from one of my postgrads." The professor hunted for his car keys. "Where are my car keys?"

"They're in your coat pocket, dear. Are you going somewhere?"

"I'm leaving for Mountain View. We may have received a signal from an extraterrestrial intelligence."

"Oh that is good news, dear. Does that mean you won't be here for lunch?"

"Don't you see, Elsie, this could be the end of everything."

"Now, don't be so pessimistic, Bert. They'll probably be good neighbors. And if they like to listen to the radio, they must be friendly. How far away are they?"

"The Pleiades, 400 light years away."

"There you are. We've nothing to worry about. They're too far away to ever reach us here on Earth."

The professor swung into his coat. Fido did his impression of a spinning barred spiral galaxy.

"Give me a minute. I'll make up a cold snack for you," said Elsie. "You can take it with you."

The professor put the dog's leash back on its hook. Fido whimpered and returned to his basket with a hangdog look.

Elsie handed the professor a lunchbox at the door. "Drive carefully, dear."

The professor hit the Freeway at speed. The rush hour hadn't started, and he arrived at Mountain View in record time. Flinging the door open, he stormed in. The Signal Monitor Room was deserted. The monitors were all playing the same tune: Hummm, rattle, hummm hummm, rattle, hummm, over and over and over. Nosecone was right. There could be no doubt about it: after countless fruitless years, SETI had finally come up with the goods! One glance at the computer's flashing lights confirmed that SETI's powerful translation app was already working on the signal.

The professor barged into the restroom. "Where are you, Nosehair?"

"I'll be out in a moment, Professor," said Brasenose from cubicle 2.

"Have you released the information to anyone?"

"No one," said the postgrad.

The professor drew his revolver and emptied it through the cubicle door.

"Why?" croaked Brasenose emerging from the cubicle, clutching his chest.

"We can't release this news," replied the professor. "If the military find out they'll be all over it like a cheap suit. You can bet your bottom dollar they'll close us down."

Professor Wheelright applied the coup de grâce and left Brasenose bleeding on the restroom floor. He returned to the Signal Monitor Room. The app was silent. It had finished the translation.

The postgrad's phone was bleeping. The professor picked it up and read the incoming Twookie message:

@Aliens Hullo planet earth. We're on our way. Should get there by Friday. LOL

CHILDREN

SINCE PASSING THROUGH THE Kuiper Belt and leaving the solar system, a little over six years earlier, Radarman Randy Raines's long-range radar screen had been mind-numbingly blank. Lulled by the constant drone of the ion drives and with limbs leadened by the unaccustomed gravity, he often nodded off towards the end of his shift.

The Radarman was asleep at his post, his chin resting on his chest, lost in his dreams and snoring gently, when the long-range radar began to bleep. Gradually, the persistent sound invaded his mind and tore down the membrane around his dreams. He awoke with a start. Instantly, his eyes were riveted to the screen, his heart beating like a bird in a snare.

"Radar to bridge."

"Go ahead radar." It was Commander Chandler.

"I'm picking up multiple signals ahead, sir."

"What kind of signals?"

"Difficult to tell, sir. They look like small objects."

"Asteroids?"

"I don't think so, sir. Too uniform for that."

"Ships?"

"Possibly, sir, but they're not moving."

"How far ahead?"

"At the limit of the equipment, say zero point six light years."

"How many targets?"

"Forty or fifty."

"I'm coming down."

Radarman Raines's mind was racing. He stared at the radar screen. There was no mistake: the upper portion of the screen was full of small blips, positioned in what appeared to be three lines. Then he blinked. The bleeping stopped abruptly and the screen was blank again.

His jaw fell. He slapped the side of the screen. Nothing. He thumped it with his fist. Still nothing. Frantically, he checked the cable feeds from the external radar dish. Nothing amiss there. Suppressing the impulse to panic, he powered up the standby system. He was still waiting for the second screen to warm up when Commander Chandler arrived.

Radarman Raines explained what had happened. The commander gave him one of his withering looks and Raines began his explanation again. He tried to use different words the second time, but it still sounded crazy. When the second screen showed nothing, the commander glared at his Radarman.

"You were asleep at your post, weren't you, Crewman?"

"No, sir. I saw—"

"I think you were asleep and you had a dream."

"Oh no, sir, really. I saw—I heard—"

"Or maybe you just imagined that you saw something."

"No, sir. I really did see multiple targets."

Commander Chandler shook his head and stroked his square chiseled chin. "It's hardly surprising, Crewman.

After years of looking at a blank screen anyone might start to imagine things. I won't report this to the captain. Take a month's leave."

***

The vast spaceship powered its way across the galaxy. Hour after hour, day after day, month after month, its cluster of huge engines drove the craft forward relentlessly through the blackness of deep space. The *Britney* was shaped roughly like a basking shark, the gaping jaws – the Primary Receptor – capturing the tiny particles of space dust which fueled the seven ion drives.

Crewman Buster 'Bonecrusher' Brown sat in his quarters tossing peanuts from his large hands into his small mouth. He was short in stature, but with a heavily muscled upper body and a small head, flat at the back and topped by a standard Spacefleet crew cut. Gloomily, he peered out of his window. It was not a real window, but a plasma screen providing a lateral view of the stars fed from a camera. The ship was traveling at unimaginable speed—over 60% light speed—and yet there was no sensation of movement at all. It was as if they were hanging motionless in space. He flicked a switch and the view was replaced by a feed from a posterior camera. This view was exactly the same. More stars. No sign of Earth, not even a hint at where the solar system might be. He didn't bother trying the anterior view: it would show more of the same. He yawned, switched off the screen and climbed wearily onto the lower bunk.

The door opened and his cabin mate entered. Crewman Fairfield Lightfoot was young and blond, thin as a pencil with acne which flared up from time to time. A mathematics graduate, awarded a rare *maxima cum laude* honors degree from the University of Wisconsin, he had been included on the mission as a last-minute replacement for somebody else.

"What's our gravity today?" Brown asked.

"One point zero-zero-three-seven-two G. That's about three-eighths of one percent above normal Earth's gravity."

"Feels a lot more."

Lightfoot laughed. He changed into his sleeping gear and clambered onto the upper bunk. "It's only a tiny fraction more than it was yesterday," he said.

"Well, I can feel every bit of it," Brown muttered. "Feels like I've put on about ten pounds."

***

Captain Banks found Commander Chuck Chandler in the navigation bay pouring over the figures.

"Butch."

"Chuck."

The usual curt greeting. The captain and his commander had developed a close understanding during several shared near-space missions and a few hairy moments. They needed few words to communicate.

"Just rechecking the figures, Captain."

"And?"

"They look fine."

Captain Banks smiled ruefully. Oh, the numbers were fine. In his mind's eye he could see their smug self-satisfied faces back at Mission Base. Anyone could see from the numbers that everything was going according to plan. He spat and a warm ball of brown saliva pirouetted sharply downwards and splattered on the floor by his boots.

The captain took a seat, and Chandler continued with his calculations. Neither man spoke for two minutes. Then the commander said: "A bit like the Jupiter trip."

"A lot longer."

After another long pause, the captain said: "What d'you reckon, Chuck?"

The commander considered for a few seconds before answering: "I think we'll be okay, Captain, barring accidents."

"And the crew?"

"That's another matter entirely, Butch. Keep six men cooped up together in a tin can for seven years—"

"Round trip fifteen."

"—without the basic necessities of life..."

"We've discussed this before, Chuck. There's bound to be tensions."

"Yes, Captain, I agree with you, but Brown and Raines—"

"Hate each other. I know. Just keep them apart as much as you can."

***

Crewmen Brown and Lightfoot were in the gym, pumping weights.

"I have a proposition for you," Brown said.

"A bet?"

"Right. I bet you that nothing important happens for the next four months."

"And by nothing important you mean what?"

"Anything at all. Anything out of the ordinary."

"I have a new zit on my nose."

"That's not important."

Lightfoot laughed. "It is to me."

"I mean something important relating to the mission."

"Like what?"

"Okay, say we get hit by a meteor—"

"And we all get killed."

"Uh-huh. Or we fly into the heart of a sun."

"And we all get killed."

"Yep. Or we get attacked by aliens with vastly superior weapons."

"Hostile aliens?"

"Yeah."

"And they kill us all?"

"Yup. Or maybe we all go space-crazy."

"And we all kill one another."

"Something like that."

"So if we survive the next four months, you win the bet?"

"Yep."

"And if we all die, then I win?"

"That's it."

"Fifty bucks?"

"Fifty bucks."

***

The ship sped on and on through interstellar space. The seven ion drives continued to build their acceleration little by little until they reached the optimum level of 1.0048G and a speed approaching 70% light.

Two weeks after that, mid-journey arrived and the crew put their pre-mission training into action. First, the engines were switched off, then, in zero gravity, all internal fittings were re-oriented for deceleration. Floors became ceilings, ceilings became floors. Commander Chandler used the lateral thrusters to turn the ship through 180 degrees, the engines were restarted, and the journey resumed. The whole process went like clockwork and took just two hours.

***

Crewman Fairfield Lightfoot was at his post in the communications room when the radio signals came through. He buzzed Crewman Brown first.

"You owe me fifty bucks," he said.

After that Lightfoot alerted Commander Millhouse Ironside.

"Are you recording?" the commander said as he stepped through the door.

"Yes, sir."

"Good man. And are you sure the signal is from the aliens?"

"Certain, sir. The source is in the neighborhood of the pulsar. Also, the signals are in the same language as the originals."

"The ones received by SETI on Earth? The spaghetti numbers?"

"Fibonacci numbers. Yes, sir."

"OK. Have you made any sense of them yet?"

"I have determined that the signal is a short message repeating on a loop."

"And the message? What does it say?"

The Crewman shook his head. "I'm sorry, Commander. It will take time to work something out."

"Right, let me know when you have it."

***

"Radar to bridge."

Crewman Brown was on long-range radar watch while his nemesis, Radarman Randy Raines, was on leave.

"Go ahead radar." It was Commander Ironside.

"I'm picking up multiple signals ahead, sir."

"What kind of signals?"

"Difficult to tell, sir. They look like small objects."

"Asteroids?"

"I don't think so, sir. Too uniform for that."

"Ships?"

"Possibly, sir, but they're not moving."

"How far ahead?"

"About one half light-year."

"How many targets?"

"I'm not sure. Three hundred, possibly."

"I'm coming down."

Crewman Brown's mind was racing. He stared at the screen. There was no mistake: the upper portion of the screen was full of small blips, positioned in what appeared to be three long lines. Then the bleeping stopped abruptly and the radar screen was blank. He blinked.

****

Crewman Lightfoot consulted the most authoritative translation of the original message received by SETI, twenty years earlier. The content of the message had been circulated widely and was well known amongst the scientific community of the entire planet.

The message began with a series of numbers: *0, 1, 1, 2, 3, 5, 8, 13, 21, 34, 55, 89, 144...* instantly recognizable as the first few terms of the Fibonacci series. This series was first highlighted by Leonardo Fibonacci of Pisa in the thirteenth century. Each number is the sum of the two previous. It is remarkable for many reasons, but principally because it has been found to occur again and again in nature.

What followed was a sequence of roughly two hundred thousand Fibonacci numbers: *0 13 55 21 0 2 34 13 89 89 233 0 5 21 8 5 144 0 34 55 377 1 0 0 3 13 55 55 0...* and so on.

It was quickly realized that the zero represented a separator which effectively divided the sequence into blocks, and it was assumed that if each number represented a letter of some unknown alphabet, then each block would represent a word. Double zeros were assumed to represent a period.

After that, progress was slow. Many attempts were made to translate the message, but without much success. Based on probability theory and the signal context, a group of statisticians from MIT claimed to have interpreted about twenty words and these were widely accepted, although a small number of eminent old-school scientists disputed their interpretation.

Many mainstream religious groups and some fringe sects came up with their own interpretations of the text. The Pope declared that the message represented a passage from a lost book of the Bible and that its meaning would never be understood until the lost book was found. The Unitarian Church of Australasia declared that the message was a map of Tasmania. By lining up the first 1,500 words in groups, so that the number 34 was placed in a vertical line, something roughly resembling a map of Tasmania could be made to appear. Unfortunately, they had no explanation for the remaining 38,500 words of the message. The Hell's Angels Alliance denounced the whole thing as a fraud perpetrated by the United States of America, a sequel to their earlier production: The Moon Landings Deception, 1969-1977. One British scientist became convinced that the message was a DNA sequence and he took to his laboratory to try and prove it.

Lightfoot made a list of the 'words' in the new message. There were only thirty of them, repeating over and over. He ran his eye down the list of words from the original message which had been interpreted and wrote down what he had.

GREETINGS / MESSAGE BEGINS

???????
DANGER
???????????
?? MESSAGE ????
?? HERE (Pulsar SGC 443)
DANGER
DANGER
GOODBYE / MESSAGE ENDS

Crewman Lightfoot gave his translation to Commander Ironside and the commander took it to the captain on the bridge.

"What do you make of it, Millhouse?"

"Beats me, Captain."

The two men stared at the message for a few moments in silence. Then the commander said: "We should send a reply."

"You reckon?"

"Well, we don't want to appear rude."

"I suppose. What should we say?"

The commander shrugged. "How about: Got your message. Be with you in about five months. Put the beer on ice. Signed Butch."

Both men laughed.

***

Commanders Chandler and Ironside were off duty.

"What's your opinion of Lightfoot?" Chandler asked.

"A greenhorn."

"Yes, but is he as clever as he's supposed to be?" Chandler added cold water to the hot stones. A plume of steam enveloped both men.

"Seems smart enough."

"He knows his math, but would he be any use to us in a tight corner?"

Ironside shrugged his broad shoulders, applying the birch twig to his back. "We'll know by the time we get back home."

"You reckon?"

"Sure."

Ironside watched, fascinated, as the steam condensed on his companion's face, rolled at high speed down his square chiseled chin and disappeared amongst the hairs of his massive chest. "I'm a bit worried about the other two," he said.

"Crewman Brown and Radarman Raines may have their differences, but they're both professionals. Neither of them will do anything to jeopardize the mission. You know that."

Chandler nodded vigorously, spraying cold droplets everywhere. "Yes, I know, but Raines seems spooked."

The two men were silent for a while, luxuriating in the hot steam.

Ironside said, "I've had to medicate Brown. I reckon his problems date back to his hallucination."

"His what?"

"His hallucination. He had a strange experience with the long-range radar."

Commander Chandler leapt to his feet. His towel fell to the floor. "What? What did you say?"

Commander Ironside laughed. "Better put that away, Chuck." Chandler seemed totally unaware of his nakedness.

"You say Brown saw something on the long-range radar? When? What did he see?"

"He thought he saw multiple targets ahead."

"Oh God! When?"

"I don't know. About six weeks ago."

Commander Chandler was suddenly white as a ghost. He sat down heavily. "Raines picked up multiple targets, too."

"When?"

"About two months ago. The images were gone by the time I got down to radar from the bridge. I thought he must have imagined them."

"It was the same with Brown. I was sure he was sleeping on duty, so I never reported it."

The two commanders looked at each other.

Ironside handed Chandler his towel. "Better put some clothes on, Chuck. We need to talk to the captain."

***

"So what d'you reckon these radar targets were?" The captain's brow furrowed seriously.

Ironside shrugged. "Who knows, Captain?"

Chandler said, "I think we've got to assume the worst."

"And what's the worst, Chuck?"

"Hostile aliens. Hundreds of ships waiting for us."

The captain turned to Ironside. "Do you agree with that assessment, Commander?"

"It's hard not to, Captain. Even if they're not hostile, we can't afford to take a chance. I mean, look at our situation. We're hurtling through space inverted—"

"Bass ackwards, you mean," Chandler interjected.

"—and with zero maneuverability. Talk about a sitting duck!"

"We do have weapons," the captain said.

Chandler laughed nervously. "We have limited weapons, Captain, and given that we can't alter our course direction, I'm not sure what good they'd be in a fight."

"What do you make of the loss of the radar signals?" The captain's question was aimed at both men.

"Some sort of cloaking technology?" Chandler suggested.

Ironside shook his head. "Their technology must be far superior to ours if they can hide a whole fleet of ships. I wouldn't fancy getting into a firefight with an enemy that we can't even see."

"If they can hide their ships, how come we saw them? Twice?" the captain said.

Commander Ironside shrugged, "Maybe their cloak failed for a short while or maybe they gave us a glimpse of their fleet to warn us off."

The captain pulled a copy of the alien message from his tunic pocket. He placed it on the table. "And what about this?" he said.

The three men re-read the message.

GREETINGS / MESSAGE BEGINS
???????
DANGER
???????????
?? MESSAGE ????

?? HERE (Pulsar SGC 443)
DANGER
DANGER
GOODBYE / MESSAGE ENDS

"There's too many DANGERs in there for my liking, Captain," Ironside said.

"And that GOODBYE sounds pretty final," Chandler added.

"What we need is more information. Chuck, how's Lightfoot getting on with translating the message?"

"He's trying, Butch, but he's reported no progress so far."

"Check with him again. Tell him it's priority one."

***

Each week for the ensuing two months, the captain and his senior staff held a meeting to consider their options. The meetings were brief, their options limited, and the outcome of each meeting was the same: no action taken.

One month from their destination, the radar signal returned.

"Radar to bridge."

"Yes, Radarman." It was the captain.

"I have multiple signals, Captain, on my long-range radar." Radarman Raines spoke in even tones that belied his state of mind.

"I'm coming down."

This time the captain made it in time to see the signals. There were hundreds of them filling the top half of the screen.

"Any idea what we're looking at, Randy?" The captain's face was grim.

"Sorry, Captain. It's just like before. Hundreds of echoes, all about the same size. Range about a quarter light year."

"They're not moving?"

"No discernible movement, sir, no."

The captain called his two commanders to the radar room, but by the time they arrived the signals had evaporated.

"You saw them, Captain?"

"Yes, Chuck. Hundreds of them, filling the upper quadrant of the screen."

"Then we must act immediately." Ironside's voice was half an octave higher than normal.

The captain shook his head. "Send a dispatch back to Earth, but take no hostile action."

"But Captain—"

"That's enough, Commander. What chance would we have against so many?" He turned to Chandler. "How long to engine shutdown, Chuck?"

"Twenty-seven days, Butch."

"And Lightfoot?"

"I haven't seen him for days."

"Talk to him. Impress on him the urgency of his work."

***

Commander Chandler ran into Crewman Lightfoot on his way to the bridge.

Lightfoot was breathless. "I've done it, sir!"

"You have a full translation?"

"I have, and I can assure you that we are among friends."

"Show me."

Lightfoot handed him a short piece of paper:

Hi there!

Take your place in the queue

Hurry!

Welcome to the event of your lifetime!

Have your tickets ready for inspection

At Pulsar centre

Hurry!

Hurry!

Enjoy the show!

The commander read through the message twice. Then he said: "Are you sure about this, Crewman?"

"Yes, sir. It was written in Latin."

"Latin."

"Yes, sir. I think whoever sent it used the most prevalent language on our planet."

"Latin."

"Yes, sir. In Fibonacci's time Latin would have been the most prevalent language on Earth."

"So, what does it all mean?"

Lightfoot handed the commander a second piece of paper. "This is my translation of the original message received by SETI. I haven't completed the translation yet, but I think what I have explains everything."

Hi there!

Announcing the event of a lifetime!

A Supernova explosion!

How often does an event like this happen in your neighborhood?

Not to be missed!

Something to tell your great great grandchildren about!

Come and see the Supernova Spectacular!

Watch the whole thing in complete safety!

Seats are limited, so make sure you have secured your tickets in time!

And remember, children are admitted free!

"So the original message was a promotion?"

"Undoubtedly. The aliens have been selling tickets to watch a Supernova explosion."

"Since the thirteenth century?"

"Yes, sir."

"And the alien ships?"

"Are queuing for seats."

"But we have no tickets!"

Lightfoot laughed. "I think that won't be a problem, sir. Children are admitted free."

INTELLIGENT DESIGN

THE MOOD IN HEAVEN was gloomy. All four Team Leaders and their senior designers were summoned to a special Project Review meeting.

The work had fallen so far behind that its projected time to completion was now anybody's guess. Many of the rank and file team members believed that the whole project would be scrapped by Senior Management before completion.

Of course, the delays were the fault of nobody in particular. Many felt that the Quality Control Department had overstepped its authority on several occasions, rejecting some designs which would have been perfectly adequate. The team working on the locomotion problem, for example, had been particularly upset when their elegant flying concept had been rejected as "too dangerous". This was a great blow, when you consider their earlier designs for locomotion, based on swimming, crawling, hopping, etc., each perfectly plausible, but all vetoed by the Quality Control Department.

The meeting started late, as God Junior had been delayed by a staff problem. Tight-lipped, He addressed the meeting :

"I have to tell you," He said in His most stentorian voice, "that Senior Management is most unhappy with progress on the project. I have been asked to convey to you all the most serious displeasure with which your work is viewed from On High."

The senior designers and Team Leaders shifted nervously in their seats. Many cast their eyes down. Some fidgeted with their papers.

"You all know how close the project is to My Father's heart, which is why, after much persuasion, He has agreed to continue to support your efforts for the time being."

There was a general sigh of relief around the table.

"However, He has asked me to make it plain to all of you that His patience is not infinite, and He is confident that you will all be able to report significant progress at the next review meeting."

God Junior paused, and looked around the table, establishing eye contact with each of the Team Leaders in turn before continuing.

"Now, I think we should press on with our review, so I will call upon our Executive Vice President for Organic Life Development to summarize the overall state of the project. Gabriel."

Archangel Gabriel was a tall, impressive figure, immaculately dressed in luminous white with gold trim. He rose and addressed the meeting without the aid of notes.

"As you all know, the project is way behind schedule. Estimates vary, but you can take it that this is certainly the longest project undertaken in the Firmament since the development of DNA, and may well break many existing records by the time it is completed."

His listeners noted the optimistic turn of phrase.

"With regard to progress so far, let me take the four main teams in turn: Firstly, we have the Sensory Input team. I believe that this team is quite close to completing its work. Their recent innovations with stereoscopic vision were quite stunning and we have functional working models for the four senses - sight, hearing, touch and smell."

Several senior project team members raised their hands to interject, but Gabriel dismissed them with a wave of his hand.

"Yes, yes, I know many of you believe there should be five or even six senses, but we will leave that discussion for the moment. Second, we have the Metabolism team, who are making great progress now, with the Endothermic model. It's good to see that your latest designs have reasonable body sizes, again, George." There were several sniggers around the table. "However, I believe that you still have a long way to go. Am I right?"

The Metabolism team had spent Ages working on the Exothermic model, before the Quality Control Department finally axed it. The main problem here was body size. Exotherms had to be enormous in order to regulate their body temperatures, and quite frankly, some of the later Exothermic body sizes produced by this team were absolutely ridiculous.

George stood up. He looked uncomfortable and quite disheveled for an angel.

"I have an outstanding team of designers, as you know, and we have always given the project one hundred and one percent effort. Our principal difficulty is the rapid rate of change of climatic conditions. It is very discouraging for the teams to have to rework their designs so often. All of our designs, even the larger ones, were practical solutions to the problems presented to us, and worked quite well..." His voice tailed off, and he sat down.

"Thank you, George. We are all aware of the difficulties imposed by climate change, as these changes affect everyone here, but I think you would agree that a design that 'worked quite well' is not good enough. Am I right, George?" He waited for a response from George, who nodded sheepishly.

"Thank you, George. Next, we come to the Locomotion and Dexterity team. This has been a major stumbling block. We have seen so many very creative and original ideas, but none of these has come near the sort of thing that we need. I should add that I personally favored the flying model at first, but I have now come around to the generally accepted view that it limits body weight too much. However, it opens up a world of possibilities for lower forms of Life, and I understand that a special design team has now been set up to concentrate on designs for flying species. As to the latest idea, I know there are radical elements amongst you who support it, but I ask you – does it look stable? And I don't think 'bipedal' is even a real word.

"Finally, we have the Internal Organs team, and while we all appreciate the great difficulties which they have to work under, the progress of this team has been abysmal. With regard to the development of the brain, all of the motor functions and sensory input links are well developed, but the higher cognitive and reasoning brain functions are still on the drawing board. Am I right, Harold?"

Harold stood up. "Yes, that is substantially correct," he said. "However, we have made some additional progress since the last review meeting. For example, the cerebral cortex..."

"Thank you, Harold," said God Junior. "We will come to the specifics later."

Harold resumed his seat, and Gabriel continued, "With regard to the development of the vocal organ, we have seen no significant progress since the squawk-screech which was presented at the meeting before last. I believe we have an agreed design for a basic hydraulic system to circulate blood round the body, and various sundry organs on the drawing board which will allow for absorption of nutrients and cleansing and reproductive functions, but it's hard to see how we are going to fit them all inside the frame. Perhaps, Harold, you and your team are contemplating a sort of portable accessories bag for carrying around any organs which cannot be fitted inside?"

There was a general howl of derision at this remark. The laughter quickly died away when the Archangel raised his hand for silence.

Harold stood up again and replied: "Well, Gabriel, you know my views on the need for organ redundancy. It would be a shame for the project to founder because of the mechanical failure of some insignificant but vital piece of equipment."

Gabriel replied: "I understand the value of organ redundancy as well as the next angel, Harold, but surely two kidneys, two livers, two hearts, two testicles and two lungs is just a bit over the top."

Harold sat down, and Gabriel resumed: "So where are we? What have we achieved so far? As I see it, the most advanced design which we have is a small furry creature which can see, hear, touch and smell. It has four legs which allow it to move about and find its food. It can convert its food directly into body heat, so it can function in the dark and in cold climates. However, it cannot think or talk, and it has very little manual dexterity."

"Thank you, Gabriel," said God Junior. "Are there any questions at this point?"

A hand shot up near the end of the table. "Yes, at the back there."

"Hector, senior designer, Herbivores. I would like to hear the Senior Project Manager's comments on Carnivores and the Food Chain concept. Speaking for myself and for my colleagues in Herbivore Design, we would like to know who originated these ideas and why they were approved."

There was a general murmur of agreement around the table. Gabriel consulted God Junior before rising to answer.

"If I recollect accurately," said Archangel Gabriel, "this item was raised several meetings ago, and I thought that it had been discussed and resolved to everyone's satisfaction then. The Food Chain concept is absolutely necessary in order to maintain the various species in balanced numbers. I cannot say who originated the idea, but I know that it was approved at the Highest Level."

George stood up. "I would just like to add," he said, "that it is quite disheartening for my designers to know that many of their best ideas will be eaten. Senior Management should be aware of the demoralizing effect which decisions like this have on the more junior members of the design teams."

Several hands were raised now. God Junior indicated one.

"Maurice. Sensory Input. What I and my colleagues object to is the Law of Natural Selection. I cannot see why the whole mechanism has to revolve around the notion of the Survival of the Fittest. How does this leave room for creative expression, for joy and beauty? Why not the Survival of the Prettiest, or Survival of the Least Offensive?"

These remarks were greeted by general laughter. God Junior answered: "Thank you, Maurice for that question. As everyone here knows, the physical dimension of the project is limited to the closed environment of the planet's surface, and is thus predicated upon inherent environmental constraints which are given expression in what we call Natural Laws. These Laws are effectively axiomatic to the orderly development of Organic Life. Without these Laws, Life could not exist, just as the Laws have no meaning or existence without Organic Life. The Law of Natural Selection is the most logical way to propagate well-adapted species at the expense of those less well equipped for survival. Does that answer your question, Maurice?"

Maurice looked a little bemused, but he nodded and sat down.

God Junior resumed: "Now, I will ask Michael, our Executive Vice President for the Fabric of the Universe to say a few words. Michael."

Archangel Michael rose to his feet. He was a tall, impressive figure, immaculately dressed in luminous white with gold trim.

"Thank you, God. I would like to start by explaining the basic principles of planetary development and environmental controls. Many of you will be familiar with these principles, but I feel it would be useful to go over them once more, starting from the Big Bang..."

***

Archangel Raphael sat at his desk, picking his teeth. He was a tall, impressive figure, immaculately dressed in luminous white with gold trim.

It had been a slow millennium. Only fifteen new species had been approved for release, and his team had completed all of the necessary work and gone off to choir practice.

As Executive Vice President in charge of General Operations, he was responsible for putting all of the approved designs into production on the planet. The Quality Control Department, while nominally independent of all other departments, operated under his jurisdiction, so he had an effective, but unofficial veto on all new designs.

He finished with his teeth, leaned back in his executive chair crossed his feet on the corner of the desk and folded his hands behind his head. He yawned and closed his eyes.

His cell phone rang.

"Raphael?"

"Oh hi, Lucifer."

"Hi. Listen, God Almighty and I visited the Quality Control Department today, and we took a look at some recently rejected designs."

Raphael's heart sank,

Lucifer continued, "We feel that there are one or two which should be given further consideration."

"Which ones?"

"Well, there's a large reptile with lots of teeth..."

"Carnivorous? With a long tail? Lives in the water?"

"That's the fellow. Looks like he might be a long term survivor."

"Okay. What else?"

"There's a sort of small furry creature with a flat beak and webbed feet…"

"You must be joking. I'm pretty sure that was just a prank by one of the juniors in Metabolism. Surely you don't believe that design is viable?"

"Well, God Almighty liked it."

Raphael groaned. "Okay, but it won't survive more than a few generations. What should we call it?"

"I don't know. How about 'Furry-flat-beaked-web-footed Platypus'?"

"Too long. How about 'Amphibian Duck-bill'?"

"Maybe. Let me leave that with you. There was something else."

"Yes?"

"We were wondering if we could give these marsupial designs a try."

"The ones with the stomach pouches?" Raphael was incredulous.

"Yes."

"But they would never survive. The whole design concept is clearly flawed…"

"Yes, you and I both know that, but He is very keen to give them a try, so I thought maybe you could find them a secluded area of their own, somewhere."

"What, you mean segregated from the other designs?"

"Yes. A large island, maybe."

"Is this another of His ideas or one of your own?"

"Mine, but He agrees with my thinking. Can you do it?"

"Yes, I suppose so."

"You *suppose* so. I'll pass your message on."

"Tell Him, yes, of course I can do it. No problem. Okay?"

"Okay. Thanks, Raphael. Bye."

Raphael ended the call and snorted angrily. That upstart was far too close to God Almighty for comfort, he thought. Will probably overreach himself some day and come to a hot and sticky end.

***

Of course, the project did reach completion, as you know, and shortly after the celebrations, Lucifer resigned and set up a rival organization of his own, taking many of the angels with him.

When Adam awoke for the first time he found himself all alone in a beautiful garden. He was a little miffed, to put it mildly, but Archangel Raphael soon corrected the oversight. He gave Adam a general anesthetic, removed one of his ribs and created Eve.

When Adam awoke for the second time he was very pleased with what he saw. It took him a few weeks to recover from the operation, and after that ... well, you know the rest of the story. It's been previously published elsewhere.

SCOUTING PARTY

THE SHIP LANDED IN darkness. After so long in space with the constant drone of the engines, they were suddenly afraid. Strapped in their individual protective pods, they reached out to each other and their fingertips touched.

Slowly, imperceptibly, the whine of the engines reduced in pitch, and their apprehension increased. The enormity of their predicament gripped their minds again.

The engines came to a complete stop. Their ears adjusted to the atmospheric pressure, and the silence engulfed them. Outside, the darkness was almost complete. Through the viewing panels, they could just make out dark shapes of tall vegetation and a slight red glow in the sky.

Their instruments told them that the atmosphere outside was breathable and the temperature was high, but within tolerance. They did not need their instruments to tell them that the gravity on the planet was well above what they were used to. Keeping their heads upright required constant small adjustments, and their arms and legs felt like lead.

Wearily, they anchored and secured the ship and busied themselves with the nearly-forgotten standard system checks designed to follow landfall. Breaking their radio silence, they transmitted a short pre-arranged message to tell those at home that they had reached their destination.

Finally they slept, clinging to one another like lost children in one of the two bunks. Even in sleep, they were aware of the strange gravity that pinned them to the bunk and seemed to pull at their lungs, making breathing difficult.

***

When they awoke, they saw that the ship was surrounded on all sides by tall green-brown vegetation. The red glow in the sky had been replaced by bright blue and white. They could not see the planet's star but could tell its rough position in the sky from the shadows. Its brightness and the size of the vegetation around the ship confirmed that it was a healthy young white dwarf star, as expected.

Using deep earth probes, they replenished their water tanks. A complete mission status check confirmed that they were in good shape. The ship was undamaged by their high speed descent through the atmosphere or by landfall. Their food reserves were high and all primary systems were fully operational. Their fuel reserves were low, but no lower than expected and they had known before takeoff that they would need to refuel the ship from the planet's resources.

The long hours of daylight were spent making preparations for the expedition, and then as darkness began to fall again, they opened the door and stepped outside.

It was hot. The sickly sweet smell of the strange trees was everywhere, and they could hear a variety of chirping, whistling and cackling sounds from the life-forms in the trees around them.

The planet's high gravity made her progress down the access ladder slow and painful. Once at the bottom of the ladder, she took a few careful steps away from the ship and turned. He was at the bottom of the ladder still clinging to the rungs. He looked terrified. She beckoned for him to join her but he refused to move, and she had to go back and comfort him before he would let the ladder go.

He checked the homing beacon. Then they took one last, long look at their ship nestling among the trees and headed into the forest.

Their progress was slow, their steps faltering through the undergrowth, but soon they came to a rough track cut through the forest. They followed this for a while, until, rounding a bend, they came upon an open green area surrounded by a metal fence. Several large black and white animals stood behind the fence. They were grotesque looking creatures, standing on four thick legs, with bodies of enormous girth. When the animals saw them they ran away in terror, each with a large pink-white sack swinging from side to side between its rear legs.

They hurried on down the track, emerging from the forest to find a paved area with crude painted markings leading away left and right.

They heard it before they saw it. A large blue metal container on wheels, with two lights at the front, roaring, belching foul-smelling smoke, rattling and shaking. They ducked down by the side of the road as it roared on by.

"What was that?" Squeed said between coughs.

"A vehicle of some sort, I suppose," replied Mool.

"Did you see any occupants?"

"I think so. Just one, but I did not get a good look at it."

"Was it like the creatures in the forest?"

"No. I do not think so, Squeed. It must have been an intelligent life form."

They both burst into a spontaneous fit of giggling.

When the giggling subsided, Squeed asked, "What did it look like?"

"Even more hideous, I would say," Mool replied.

Squeed groaned, and she wrapped an arm around his shoulders his chest and his waist to comfort him.

They walked on, following the road in the direction taken by the vehicle. Soon, they came to a dwelling. It was small and rectangular, with a pointed roof and was made of a hard, rock-like substance. There were lights shining through some of the rectangular viewing panels. Cautiously, they approached and peered inside one of the lower panels.

The creatures inside were indeed hideous. There were two of them, standing upright and walking around with short thick limbs and thick necks, their bodies covered all over with loose-fitting colored material. Their features were particularly repellent. Their mouths were wide, the nasal orifices mounted in large protruding organs in the centre of their faces. They had strange protrusions on either side of their heads, whose purpose neither Mool nor Squeed could guess. Most repellent of all were their eyes which were very small and set deep in sunken sockets below a protruding forehead. Their heads were covered in a strange downy material of variable length.

Mool stood on a small metal cylinder at the side of the dwelling and peered inside. She could see a third creature preparing for bed. This creature was uncovered, and Mool was immediately aware that this was a female, although she could not have explained how she knew. The creature's skin was pink-white, her short, thick body curiously rounded and curved. She carried two large sacks on her chest that wobbled as she moved.

The female creature turned, saw Mool peering in through the window, and screamed. Mool dropped to the ground, knocking the lid from the cylinder with a loud clatter. Squeed helped Mool to her feet and they hurried away to hide in the undergrowth.

A door opened and one of the creatures emerged carrying what looked like a weapon of some kind. He shouted something and fired the weapon with a loud bang into the darkness. Crouched in the bushes, Mool and Squeed covered their ears. The creature shouted again into the darkness and went back inside, closing the door.

Continuing their journey along the road for a while, the sky began to lighten. They crossed several empty fields and vaulted a hedge before emerging in a quiet tree-lined avenue. Satisfied that they were well-concealed from view, they took some food before laying down in the short vegetation to sleep.

***

"You did what?" roared Sheriff Johnson.

"I called the FBI in Phoenix. I have a cousin whose father-in-law has a fishing buddy who knows somebody related to..."

"Why didn't you call me first?" Sheriff Johnson was red in the face. He sat at his desk, the telephone receiver in his left hand, his right hand resting on the butt of his revolver in its holster.

"I tried, but I got a busy signal. I guess you were tied up."

"Okay, okay. Exactly what did you tell them?"

"I told them about the radio signal I picked up."

"From outer space?"

"Yes. I think so. It was on a very high frequency and it sounds like nothing on Earth."

"And what did the FBI say?"

"They're sending someone over this afternoon."

Sheriff Johnson groaned. "All right, Schneider. Bring me the tape recording."

"But the FBI man told me not to. . ."

"Never mind what he said. Just make sure you bring it to me first. Will you be in town today?"

"Yes, I'll be there in about an hour."

"Great. Bring me that tape."

He slammed the receiver down and buzzed the intercom. Deputy Kline came in.

"Melissa, I want you to do something for me," said the sheriff. Melissa began to unbutton her blouse. "No, Melissa. Not that. I want you to go out to the Harris place. They reported a prowler last night. Take a look round and report back, okay?"

***

The FBI man sat in his new Ford Taurus. He had cleared the city suburbs and hit the freeway just ahead of schedule. He smiled at the sight of the traffic, all headed the other way, into town.

His radio was tuned to WXCY, the local minority station with a target audience of the young, white collar workers of Yuma City and County. The music was mostly country, which he was indifferent to, but he enjoyed the irreverent anti-establishment jibes and bawdy jokes of the DJ.

He positioned the car in the middle lane at fifty-five MPH, switched on cruise control and settled himself comfortably in his seat. The DJ put on the latest Billy Ray Cyrus track.

His cell phone rang. It was Carter, his Area Manager.

"Where are you?" The tone was accusatory.

"On the freeway, sir, heading south."

"Following up that radio signal from Hicksville?"

"Yes, sir. I left a note on your desk. A radio ham from Silverdale recorded an indecipherable signal of possible alien origin."

"I don't recall authorizing a field trip. One yokel radio ham is hardly worth getting excited about."

"There have also been a number of promising reported UFO sightings in the general area south of Yuma, sir." This was a white lie. There had been exactly two reported sightings.

"Hmm. Okay, but I want your monthly surveillance reports on my desk by close of play tomorrow. Is that clear?"

"That shouldn't be a problem, sir. I'll sort that out in the morning."

He terminated the call and smiled to himself. Carter was really in no position to interfere.

Thirty minutes later, he turned off the freeway and followed a minor road to the entrance of the exclusive Silverdale Oak Woods Golf and Country Club. He parked his car, unloaded his golf clubs from the trunk, and went in search of the locker room.

***

Harry Schneider was in love. Admittedly, the object of his affections was barely aware of his presence, but not even that could dampen the general feeling of elation that he had had for the past few weeks. Ever since he had danced with Melissa Kline at the weekly two-step session in Gomez taverna. Well, he couldn't say that he had actually danced *with* her, line-dancing being more of a communal pastime, but he had danced in the same room as her, and once or twice during the evening, she had brushed against him.

He hummed a popular two-step melody to himself. He fancied it was called "Saddles 'n' Boots" or possibly "Boots 'n' Saddles".

His nearly new pickup hurtled towards town at high speed. For amusement, and with the natural exuberance of youth, Harry tried to negotiate each bend in the road without touching the brakes. Luckily, there was very little traffic in either direction and Harry made it to Silverdale with the loss of just one small prairie dog and a few millimeters of rubber from his nearly new tires.

He pulled up outside the sheriff's office, jumped from the vehicle and bounded inside.

Melissa was out on a job, so he had to shelve for another day his carefully prepared devil-may-care casual opener. Deputy Mooney ushered him straight in to Sheriff Johnson's office.

"Come in, Schneider. Sit," said the sheriff. "Now, where's this tape?"

Harry handed him the unmarked tape, and the sheriff put it in his tape recorder. "I hope this is on the level and you're not jerking my wire, Schneider," he said as he pressed the PLAY button.

The sheriff played the tape over several times. What he heard was a voice, but he could not make out any distinct words, and the language and dialect were totally unfamiliar. The pitch of the voice was also strange.

He nodded to Harry Schneider. "It certainly sounds pretty weird. What do you make of it, Harry?"

"I never heard anything like it, Sheriff. Perhaps the FBI'll be able to decode it."

"Listen, son," said the sheriff. "I don't think we really want the FBI involved in this, do we? I mean, where's the percentage in that? Look at it this way, Harry. If the tape is genuine—"

"It's no fake. . ."

"No. No. I know it's for real. What I mean is, if it's really from outer space this could be the biggest thing to hit this town since the dairy co-op was set up in 1955. Think of the publicity, the tourists."

"You mean there might be money in it?"

"Fortunes could be made, son, fortunes. Mark my words. This could be the biggest newspaper story since. . .since. . ."

"Watergate?" suggested Harry helpfully, his euphoria waning.

"Yes, whatever. How many real genuine alien space signals have been recorded?"

Harry shook his head.

"I'll tell you how many. None. Zip. Squat. This tape is unique, boy."

"I suppose so. But the FBI have a man on the way already."

"Yes, but he doesn't have to get to hear the tape, does he?"

"Doesn't he?" The knot forming in Harry's stomach told him he was losing control of the situation.

***

Emily Harris opened the door and led Deputy Melissa Kline into the kitchen. Emily's husband, Newt, and their son, Newt junior were waiting for them.

"Where's Quentin?" said Newt senior.

"The sheriff is occupied. He sent me to investigate," said Melissa.

"Yeah. Right," said Newt junior.

"Be quiet, Junior," said Emily.

Melissa sat down opposite Newt junior. His eyes were transfixed on her light brown standard issue deputy's shirt that barely restrained her ample bosom.

"Tell me what happened last night," she said.

"I told Quentin. We had a prowler," said Newt senior.

"Maybe it was the Mormons. They have been seen around the area," said Melissa.

"No. I don't think it was the Mormons," said Newt senior, shaking his head.

"Well, did you get a good look at him?" asked Melissa.

"No, but we heard 'em," said Newt senior.

"I saw one of them," said Emily.

"There was more than one?"

"Well I can't be sure," said Emily.

"Couldn't tell. It was dark," said Newt junior, helpfully.

"You said you saw one of them, Emily," said Melissa.

"Oh, you don't want to go into that, honey," said Newt senior. "Just you check outside for footprints and that. Never mind what she thought she saw."

"But I did see one of them. At the window," Emily insisted.

"Which window?" said Melissa. "This one or one at the front of the house?"

"Upstairs," said Emily.

"You saw the prowler at an upstairs window," said Melissa. "Is there a ladder outside?"

Emily and Newt senior exchanged a quick glance.

"No. There are no ladders," said Newt senior. "I told you. Pay her no heed. She's just a knucklehead woman."

"I see," said Melissa, although she didn't. "Well, what did he look like? Was he wearing a suit?"

"She," said Emily.

"I beg your pardon?" said Melissa.

"It was a she. A female," said Emily.

"A girl. Good. Now we're getting somewhere. Did you recognize her?"

"No. No. She wasn't. . . from around here."

"So what did she look like?"

"Silver," said Emily.

"Silver," echoed Melissa.

"Yes. And sort of shiny, with big eyes."

"Big eyes."

"Yes. Big, buggy eyes," said Emily, desperately. Newt junior began to wail. Newt senior whacked him across the back of the head and Junior ran out of the room.

"Okay. Anything else? Any distinguishing marks or tattoos?"

"No. Not that I recall. Let me get you something, Melissa. A coffee, perhaps?"

Melissa declined the coffee and left. Easing her ample frame into the patrol car, she flicked on the radio. "Deputy Kline to base. Are you receiving?"

"Loud and clear, Melissa." It was Deputy Mooney.

"Is the sheriff there, Mort? Let me talk to him."

"Okay. Hold on, Melissa."

Mort Mooney fetched the sheriff from his office.

"Just sit tight, Harry," said the sheriff. "This won't take a minute."

The sheriff sat on the corner of Mort's desk and picked up the radio handset.

"Melissa? Come in."

"Hi Sheriff. I am leaving the Harris place now. Nothing much to go on, but it sounds to me like it might have been the Mormons."

"The Mormons."

"That's right. Possibly more than one of them. Dressed in silver suits. Oh, and one of them was a girl."

"Did you say a girl?"

"Yes, sir. A tall girl."

"How tall?"

"Well I'm not sure, maybe eight or ten feet."

The sheriff sighed. "Come on in, Melissa, I think there's a fault on your radio."

"Roger, Sheriff. Over and out."

Sheriff Johnson went back into his office. Harry was sitting with his arms crossed tightly across his chest.

"What a noodle-brain," said Sheriff Johnson. "I expect she'll make someone a wonderful wife, someday. Now, Harry. About this tape. How do you think we should proceed?"

"Well," said Harry, "I think I should put it somewhere safe, for the moment."

The sheriff took the tape from the machine, dropped it into a desk drawer and turned the key.

"No, son, I think I should look after the tape, don't you?"

"If you think that would be best."

"I think so, son." The sheriff was opening the door.

"Okay, Sheriff. But what will I say to the FBI man when he comes looking for it?"

"You could say you lost it." The sheriff ushered Harry through the open door.

"Or accidentally recorded over it," suggested Harry, helpfully.

"Good boy, Schneider. Drive carefully," said the sheriff. He closed the door and disappeared back into his office.

***

On the advice of his local club professional, and at great expense, the FBI man had recently invested in a new set of Callaway Big Bertha woods and matching irons. He found them a little short in the shaft and somewhat light for his liking, but he was determined to persist with them.

Ever since he had taken up the game in high school, he had been fighting a natural slice. In discussions with his friends, he referred to it euphemistically as a "fade", but in all honesty his ability to misdirect his shots was unparalleled in the modern game.

His first drive whistled down the centre of the fairway, turned sharp right and hurtled into the rough under some trees.

"This is a provisional ball," he said to nobody in particular and put another ball on the tee.

The second ball followed exactly the same trajectory as the first. He considered reloading again, but he was low on ammunition. He headed off down the fairway.

He found the second ball. It was sitting quite well on a patch of rough flattened by a large sleeping animal of some kind. He lined up his next shot to the green. It looked like the perfect distance for a seven iron, if he could somehow negotiate his way through the trees.

***

Harry Schneider set out from the sheriff's office on his way home. At about the same time, Deputy Melissa Kline started the patrol car and headed back to town.

Harry reached into his breast pocket, extracted the precious tape, and dropped it on the seat beside him. He would miss his favorite Dolly Parton recording, but it couldn't be helped.

Deputy Kline drove skillfully, but carefully and only slightly above the legal speed limit. Harry Schneider drove like a madman in love, taking the bends at suicidal speeds and using his brakes as little as possible.

They met on a particularly dangerous stretch of road that ran alongside the Silverdale Oak Woods Golf & Country Club. The accident probably would not have happened if Squeed and Mool had not chosen that moment to vault over the hedge and careen across the road in front of Harry's pickup.

He managed to avoid the aliens, but he caught the patrol car a sickening blow at the front left headlight, sending it into a crazy spin. The pickup rebounded backwards, turned on its side and came to rest in a hedge at the side of the road.

Harry remained unconscious for fifteen minutes or so. When he awoke, he staggered over to where the patrol car lay crumpled and steaming in a ditch.

Pulling Melissa from the car, he carried her to a safe distance and sat with her by the side of the road, cradling her head in his lap until help arrived.

When Melissa opened her eyes, she was in pain. Her left leg was broken. Bloodied and dirty, Harry Schneider held her and spoke in reassuring tones. In spite of the pain, she felt protected and loved and found a warm corner of her heart for Harry.

***

The FBI man sat by Harry Schneider's bed in the hospital.

"I had it with me in the pickup," Harry said. "It should be there, still."

"Well, I searched the pickup and the surrounding area. There was no sign of it."

"Sorry, I can't help you." Harry lay back in the hospital pillows, a smile of utter contentment on his face.

The FBI man gave up and went back to the city. His surveillance reports were on Area Manager Carter's desk by lunchtime. He put the whole episode out of his mind, and went on to reduce his handicap to a respectable fifteen over the following five years.

***

Mool and Squeed strapped themselves in and started their engines. They had extracted the two main ingredients needed to regenerate fuel for their engines from a large, fresh cowpat. The minute metallic grains from the magnetic tape thrown from the pickup provided the final ingredient.

The ship rose into the sky and streaked off towards the stars. As soon as they were out of range of the planet, Mool called in to make their report.

"Unit 23 calling from sector 733."

"Come in Unit 23. Report."

"Planet 733.3 is habitable, but unsuitable for our purposes. Gravity is too high."

"Is it inhabited?"

"Yes, sir. There are intelligent life forms. They are hideously ugly and quite mad."

"Please explain, Unit 23."

"They employ primitive ground-based vehicles that are lethal and pollute their own atmosphere with noxious gases."

"Explain how these vehicles are lethal."

"They have no in-built anti-collision force fields."

"What about proximity detectors?"

"None of those either."

"Their technology is primitive, then."

"Yes, but they have advanced weapons."

"Explain."

"They have a portable weapon that can propel small, hard missiles around corners."

"How small?"

"Too small to support a flight guidance system."

"Interesting. You have evidence?"

"I have two nasty bruises," said Squeed.

"And we have one of the missiles," said Mool.

"Hold it up to the viewer."

Mool held up the small missile. It was white and spherical, its surface covered all over in mysterious, small dimples.

PULCHRITUDINATOR

I PLUGGED IN THE apparatus and switched it on. Soon the servos were humming like a litter of warm cats.

"What'sh your device called?" said Prince Ruprecht.

"I call it the Pulchitrudinator, mark IV, your majesty," I replied.

He squinted up at me, rolling his good eye. "What doesh it do?"

"It beautifies ugly things."

"Show me. Show me NOW."

I positioned the apparatus with the nozzle pointed at the window, locked the wheels, and adjusted the targeting parameters of the rangefinder. I turned the Master Switch to Standby and the diodes lit up one by one. When all eight functions showed Green for GO, I disengaged the safety mechanism. "Keep your eye on that ugly grey building over there, your eminence," I said.

He shuffled over to crouch by the other window, dragging his bad leg behind him. The pale London sunlight reflected off his strangely-pointed head and clawed talons, casting distorted alien shadow shapes across the bare floorboards.

"Whish one?" he said.

"The ugly squat one."

"I shee it, I shee it," he said gleefully.

"Right, now watch carefully, your princeliness …"

I turned up the power. The machine's hum became a drone; the drone became a whine, and then a scream. At full throttle I set the Master Switch to Operate. The pulsing klaxon sounded and the LED flashed its warning. "Stand Clear, Stand Clear, Machinery Operating."

I flipped the big red switch marked EXECUTE.

There was a blinding flash, a puff of smoke and a clap of thunder. When the smoke cleared, the ugly grey building was gone, in its place a beautiful, sleek tower of steel and glass shaped like a giant gherkin.

"That wasth twuly incwedible!" the prince drooled. "I wanth you to do ith again. Only thish thime I wanth you tho do ith tho me."

"Your supremeness," I said. "The device has never been tested on living flesh. I've no way of knowing what might happen if—"

"I don'th care," he slobbered.

I persisted. "You do realize that I have no antidote, no 'undo' button, no means or mechanism for reversing the process."

Snarling, he snapped his fangs at me. "Justh do ith. I'll take Weshpwonshibility for whatheveh happensh."

Hastily, I drew up a waiver, indemnifying me, my family, my antecedents and my descendants in perpetuity from all damages arising etcetera, etcetera. He signed it in triplicate, affixing the royal seal.

I found his majesty a chair and he placed his princely rear end on it. Then I pointed the apparatus nozzle at him and locked the wheels. I set the targeting parameters to 10 feet and switched the device Master Switch ON. When all eight functions showed Green, I disengaged the safety mechanism. As I turned up the power the machine's hum became a drone, a whine, a scream.

At full throttle I shouted at him, "You're absolutely sure about this, your worshipfulness?"

"Justh geth on wish ith!" he shouted back. "Should I face the machine or thurn my pwofile?"

"I've no idea, your highness," I replied. "Here goes nothing."

I set the Master Switch to Operate. The pulsing klaxon sounded and the LED flashed its warning. "Stand Clear, etcetera."

With trembling fingers I closed my eyes and flipped the big red EXECUTE switch.

There was a blinding flash and a rumble like distant thunder. When I opened my eyes Prince Ruprecht was gone. A fat, glistening toad sat preening itself on the chair.

"Cwoak!" said the prince.

SNUGGLESUIT

THE IDEA CAME TO him one morning in bed. Marjorie had gone out to work, and Charles was floating in that delicious semiconscious netherland, clinging to the receding hem of sleep's nightgown. Those arctic fishermen popped into his head, you know – the ones in that ad who use moisturizing cream to keep their hands soft. The idea hit him, fully formed, the moment he switched off his electric blanket.

Charles was wide awake and out of the bed in an instant. He dressed quickly, forgetting to clean his teeth, and charged down the stairs to the kitchen.

He put the kettle on.

By the time the kettle had boiled he had sketched out a rough technical design and identified the basic raw materials, taking into account the demands of the arctic winter and safety requirements. A number of possible names for the product came to him, complete with advertising slogans. Rough production costs provided an estimated selling price and mark-up per unit. He resisted the temptation to work out the prospects for gross income. Instead, he began a list of suitable sales outlets, while absent-mindedly pouring orange juice over his corn flakes, putting marmalade in his tea, and buttering his toast on the wrong side.

***

First thing on the agenda after breakfast was to build a prototype.

He picked out one of his old suits – a remnant of his life in employment. Then he dove into the cupboard under the stairs. This was his Aladdin's cave, where he stored all his basic supplies: plumbing and electrical bits and pieces, small off cuts of wood, jars of nails, assorted screws, nuts, bolts and washers. Here lay the remnants of past inventions and tools that he was unlikely ever to use, like a spirit-level, a slide-rule, a set of Allen keys, a bag of brass somethings that he thought might be grommets, and all those other nameless widgetty things, original purpose unknown, that might be useful some day.

It wasn't long before he had assembled everything he needed: The suit, a ball of twine, a short length of electric cable, a pile of wire coat-hangers and an electric plug.

First, he dismantled twelve or thirteen coat-hangers, converting them into more or less straight lengths of wire. He spread the suit jacket out on the floor and covered it with the coat-hangers in a rough grid design, using the twine to assemble the wire grid in handy sections. Once this stage was completed, he unstitched the lining of the jacket, inserted the wire mesh, and replaced the stitches.

Some critical calculations followed. Complicated math yielded the mutual induction of the metal lattice. This provided the outward flux of the electric field vector which he knew had to be balanced with the potential across all points of intersection; too little power and it wouldn't work; too much and the whole thing would almost certainly overheat. The transformer out of Marjorie's hairdryer was just right. Cobbling together a suitable connector from some loose copper wire, he connected it up and added the cable and plug.

The prototype jacket was complete. He put it on.

It was slightly uncomfortable around the chest and he couldn't move his arms much. His shoulders and elbows were more or less frozen in position. He knocked over a lamp and several small ornaments before he got the hang of moving around, and he had to turn sideways to go through doorways, but these were all minor technical details that he would sort out later.

The moment of truth had arrived. Taking a deep breath and with a trembling hand, he plugged the prototype into the electric socket in the wall. For a moment or two nothing happened. Then Charles had the strangest feeling. There was a tingling sensation in his chest and he felt light. It was as if the suit had relieved him of some of his weight. Seconds later he heard a faint sizzling sound and the jacket began to smoke at the back. The sizzling became a louder crackling, followed almost immediately by a violent bang and a flash from the wall socket.

As soon as Charles realized what was happening, he threw off the flaming jacket and his smoldering shirt and beat out the flames with a cushion.

***

By the time Marjorie came home for lunch, the marketing campaign had been planned out and he was working on his third prototype. Several derivative products had sprung to mind, each more or less complete with outline product designs and rough financial projections. He opened the door dressed only in his briefs.

"Hello, Marjorie," said Charles. "Guess what I've been doing."

She pursed her lips. "I dread to think, Charles. Put some clothes on." She pushed past him and went into the kitchen. The dishes from Charles's breakfast lay unwashed on the table.

"Charles," she roared, "the kitchen's a mess. And where's my lunch?"

Charles appeared in the kitchen doorway wearing one of his old suits. Marjorie looked at him with a puzzled expression on her face. The suit seemed lumpier than usual and not in the usual places, and Charles was standing in a peculiar way, his arms outstretched like a droopy scarecrow, his legs locked at the knees.

"This is my Snugglesuit, honey-bunch. D'you like it? I've been working on it all morning."

"Don't honey-bunch me, you useless oaf." She ground her teeth. "Take off that ridiculous suit and tidy up the kitchen."

By the time Marjorie left to return to work, Charles had succeeded in explaining absolutely nothing about his latest invention, but he was quite clear about his shortcomings as a bread winner and what was expected of him as a house husband.

***

Sitting in the kitchen that evening after supper, Charles tried again to explain his electric suit to Marjorie. He started at the beginning with the arctic fisherman and his initial inspiration, but before he had gotten as far as the first mishap, Marjorie was snoring softly, her large bosom rising and falling rhythmically, a lock of hair draped across her snub nose.

She awoke with a start and retired to bed. Charles remained in the kitchen. He wanted to spend some time checking out Canadian patenting costs and formulating plans for the international launch of the product, probably in New York and Vancouver, or Anchorage, perhaps...

"Charles!" Marjorie's voice was at full pitch. "Charles. What have you done with my electric blanket?"

"Ah, yes. I've been meaning to tell you about that, Marjorie dear. Prototype seven—"

"I don't want to hear any more about your stupid inventions, Charles. Just put it back on my bed this instant."

***

Over the next few days, Charles made steady progress, extrapolating the first year's sales into years two, three and four, and drafting the initial press release. He paid a visit to his tailor and picked out an attractive pin-stripe material for the first launch model.

Charles turned his mind to the problem of mobility. Within a week, he had perfected a battery-powered prototype jacket, built from the remains of his own electric blanket. He referred to it as a jacket, but in reality it looked more like one of Clint Eastwood's ponchos. It was powered by a twelve-volt car battery, the control knob, complete with orange flashing light, positioned on the left shoulder.

It was at about this time that the snags began to appear. The basic idea was sound enough, and he could regulate his body temperature with ease. However, there was the difficulty of carrying the battery, and he found that the suit's performance was unpredictable in the rain. Also – and strangest of all – the jacket had an annoying habit of riding upwards, often rolling itself up and tucking itself under his armpits.

This last problem was a real puzzler, and Charles set about solving it straight away. First, he took some measurements with his voltmeter. To his amazement, he discovered that the electric power passing through the jacket was far in excess of that being input by the battery. Either that or his math was in error somewhere. He checked and double-checked everything, but could find no mistakes in his calculations. The plain fact was that his electric suit seemed to be generating power by some unknown means and without the expenditure of any identifiable fuel.

In desperation, he put the jacket on, strapping the bottom securely to the tops of his legs, and turned the control up to 'Hi'. To his dismay, the jacket lifted him slowly off the ground. His feet were two feet above the carpet when the cable attaching the battery was extended to its limit and he came to a halt. He turned the control down a couple of points and slowly returned to the ground.

He tried several more tests and discovered that with two car batteries attached and a longer cable it was virtually impossible to keep his feet on the floor. The jacket seemed to have a mind of its own, and even with the control at 'Lo' it could lift both him and the batteries off the floor, right up to the ceiling.

Finally, he had to admit that his project had failed. With tears in his eyes, he dumped the remains of his suits and the coat-hangers in the dustbin, on top of the burnt-out cushions and the broken ornaments, and started on last night's washing up. He tried to put the whole sorry episode out of his mind, but he was haunted by the image of that brave fisherman, smooth of hand, but shivering in the bitter cold of the arctic winter.

***

That evening, Marjorie was particularly disagreeable. Her hairdryer wasn't working and she'd had a bad day at the scrapyard. Charles wasn't in the best of moods himself and they had a flaming row. He wasn't sure exactly what triggered it, but it started shortly after she discovered his suits, her cushions and the broken ornaments in the dustbin. She called him a worthless nincompoop and a parasite; he called her a nagging witch; she told him exactly where he belonged on the food chain – somewhere between a sponge and a sea-slug; he said she had the disposition of a wasp and a face like a weasel. After that the argument got really serious and Marjorie starting throwing things.

Over the weekend she made his life hell. She screeched at him constantly during the day and resisted all his attempts at reconciliation at night. She seemed particularly upset about her hairdryer and the fact that he no longer had a serviceable suit to wear, pretty much eliminating any remaining prospect of ever finding himself a job. And when she moved the rug and found the burn marks in the carpet, he thought she was going to explode.

Charles did his best to weather the storm. He did everything he could to pacify her, cleaning the house from top to bottom and cooking all her favorite meals, but nothing worked.

After two weeks, Marjorie stopped talking to him altogether. She took to sleeping in the spare room downstairs.

That was when something snapped inside Charles's head.

He waited until she was sound asleep. Then he crept into her room. She was lying on her back, snoring gently. Using a stout piece of rope, he strapped her securely to the bed. He tied one car battery to the head and the other to the tail of the bed. Then he connected up the batteries and the hairdryer transformer to her electric blanket, and strapped the control knob and orange light to one of the bedknobs.

He wheeled Marjorie, still snoring gently, onto the front lawn, and turned the control knob up to 'Hi'. The bed rose slowly off the ground, gathering speed as it went. Charles watched until the orange flashing light had disappeared into the darkness above the trees. Then he went back inside and slept like a stone.

BARTLETT REBOOTED

Fnnnff

"What did he say?"

"It sounded like Fnnnff."

Bartlett was lying on his back on a rough wooden table. He was buck naked, his eyes open, unblinking, staring at the ceiling. He was not breathing. His limbs were stiff as pokers, which was hardly surprising given that they were recovering from recent rigor mortis.

A box the size and shape of a shoebox sat perched on his chest. The box connected to an oxygen cylinder and wires from the box ran up Bartlett's nostrils.

The professor made a slight adjustment to the oxygen release valve. "Ask him again, Smedley," he said.

Smedley manoeuvred his huge bulk closer to the table. "Doctor Bartlett, what is your name?"

Gnnnnngh

"No, that's not *right*." The professor put his mouth to Bartlett's ear and raised his voice. "Try again, Doctor. Your name is...?"

Nothing.

Cardew the postgrad sniggered. "I don't think he heard you, Professor."

A long slow tremor ran through Bartlett's body, starting with his feet and moving up towards his chest.

"I think we need more water, Cardew."

"Right you are, Professor." Cardew picked up a galvanised bucket and poured water over Bartlett's legs and feet.

"Pour it on his head, you idiot, not his feet."

"Give it here." Smedley snatched the bucket from Cardew's grasp and emptied it over Bartlett's head.

Shhhmooooooooo, Bartlett gurgled.

"That sounded better," the professor shouted. "Say that again, Bartlett."

Nnnnggrhh

***

The three academics retired to a corner of the laboratory and Cardew put the kettle on.

"It looks hopeless," Cardew mumbled to Smedley, dropping three tea bags into the kettle.

"Nonsense, Cardew." The professor's hearing was as sharp as any bat's. "Have a little patience. It's bound to take time."

"It's been a week already," said Smedley.

"Six days, and he *is* talking."

"He's not making much sense."

"His vocal chords could be damaged. We can't be sure."

Cardew adjusted the spectacles on his nose. "And what of his brain, Professor?" Lifting the lid from the kettle, he poured in a quart of milk.

"His brain is perfect, young man. You'll see."

"Yes, but we've run out of time." Smedley produced a half-melted Mars bar from his pants pocket and began to unpeel it.

"We have the rest of today and tomorrow morning."

"He'll be here at ten," said Smedley, licking his fingers.

"Well there you are, then. We have at least fifteen hours."

Smedley bit his lip. "Is there no way you can postpone the visit? Maybe you could say you've caught something horrible – the plague, maybe, or a really bad head cold."

The professor shook his head. "Not necessary. I've told you before, there's no way the Military will pull the plug on this one, not now that the Secretary for Defense has got wind of it."

When they had finished their tea, they returned to find Bartlett's head turned to the left. As they approached, Bartlett fixed the wiry Cardew with a bird-like stare.

"Look, he's moved his head!" the professor whispered.

Smedley chuckled. "I think he's taken a fancy to you, Cardew."

"I see what you mean," said the professor. "Better fetch more water, and make it cold."

Bartlett's eyes followed Cardew's lissom figure as he hurried from the room.

"Bartlett!" The professor shouted. He snapped his fingers. "I'm over here, Bartlett. Look at me, Bartlett. Do you know who I am?"

Gggggggrrrroooooooooo

"That's right! Professor Gordon. Listen to this, Smedley! He said my name."

Cardew came running back carrying half a bucket of water.

The professor waved his hands in front of Bartlett's face. He snapped his fingers again, and shouted, "Bartlett, Bartlett. Look at me, Bartlett. WHO AM I?"

Ffnnnnfnngh

***

The man from the Pentagon arrived at nine o'clock on the dot. Cecil Footprint was on the wrong side of thirty but the right side of forty. His small snub nose and weak chin tucked in under his prominent brow suggested a face carved from a solid block of wood, like an African ceremonial mask. His clothing was remarkable only insofar as it was identical in every detail to what Bartlett, whom Smedley had dressed for the occasion, was wearing: a suit of worsted wool in charcoal gray, one of those shirts with red stripes and a white detachable collar, a red striped tie and sensible shoes.

Bartlett stood stiffly against the wall where Smedley and Cardew had put him.

"This is the, ah, subject?" Footprint said.

"This is Doctor Bartlett. Say hello to Mr. Footprint, Bartlett," said the professor somewhat optimistically.

Bartlett's unblinking eyes latched on to his visitor. He said nothing.

"As you can see," said the professor, "he is well aware of your presence."

Footprint took a half-step back. "What's that under his shirt, strapped to his chest?"

"That's his life-support apparatus. It's a small box full of electronic instruments that control the flow of oxygen to his brain."

"Doesn't the brain extract its oxygen from blood?"

"Normally, yes, but we use a different medium to carry oxygen to the brain."

"And this contraption of yours does that?"

"Yes."

"And the medium?"

"A special secret concoction of my own. It's only a temporary fix, of course. The brain needs oxygenated blood to function properly."

"Secret, you say?" Footprint made a face like a prep school teacher disappointed in one of his pupils.

"Yes. Its patent is pending."

Footprint scratched his head. "Can you get him to say something?"

"Yes, of course. Bartlett, tell Mr. Footprint what you have been doing this morning."

Bartlett said nothing.

"Try speaking to him yourself," the professor suggested.

The man from the Pentagon took a cautious step forward. "Footprint," he said, "Department of Science and Technology." He raised a hand, palm forward. "I come in peace."

"Take me to your leader," muttered Smedley.

Bartlett said nothing. Then he winked.

"Did he wink at me?" Footprint said.

"Yes. I think he likes you," said the professor.

"I see," said Footprint. "So you have made some progress."

"Indeed. His speech has been a little slow in coming, but some of his other functions seem to be recovering well."

"He seems to be shrinking," Footprint said as Bartlett's feet slowly slid forward and his legs bowed the wrong way at the knees. Cardew stepped forward and wedged Bartlett's feet with his own, whereupon Bartlett began to bend forward slowly from the waist, like a limp stick of celery.

"He's a little tired," the professor explained. "He was up half the night."

"Oh?" Footprint raised an eyebrow. "Doing what?"

"Playing pool." "Watching television," Smedley and Cardew said simultaneously.

With not a little difficulty, Smedley and Cardew folded Bartlett into a chair.

Footprint took a seat and opened his briefcase. He pulled out a notepad and pen. Frowning, he said, "Are you sure this is working, Professor?"

"No question. Can't you see how interested he is in everything around him?"

"He does seem alert," Footprint conceded. "But he says very little."

"Oh he's just shy," said the professor. "He's normally quite the chatterbox."

"Right. A chatterbox, you say." He wrote in his notebook.

"Quite."

"What does he talk about?"

"The weather, the stock market, world politics, that kind of thing."

"I see." He made another note on his pad.

"Yes, he is something of a free thinker when it comes to politics—"

"A radical?"

"No, no. Nothing like that. If anything, I'd say he's more conservative than most. He believes in democracy, and free speech, the right of citizens to bear arms, the deterrent value of capital punishment, human rights and so on."

Footprint scribbled furiously. "Anything else?"

"He is a committed scientist, of course."

"So he would approve of the program?"

"Well, he was my number one."

"I thought Smedley was your number one."

"Smedley was my number two. He took over from Bartlett after the accident."

"And Bartlett's contribution was?"

"He was – is – a social anthropologist by training. I expect you know that. His most recent work was with the pygmies of central Colorado. He had just completed a study of the habits and customs of the pygmies *post-mortem*."

"Post-mortem habits?"

"Customs. Burial rites, supernatural beliefs – that sort of thing."

"And how has that been of assistance?"

"Head-shrinking."

"Head-shrinking?"

"Indeed, yes. As you may know, the Colorado pygmies invariably resort to shrinking the heads of their departed sportsmen."

"Ah yes, I've heard something about that. They place the severed head in a prominent position in the home, creating a shrine dedicated to the memory of the departed loved one. I understand it's their way of honoring their dead heroes."

"Quite. But Bartlett discerned a more interesting motivation behind these practices."

"I have read that some experts believe the more primitive Colorado people actually *worship* their dead football players."

"Yes, especially the quarterbacks. But even more interesting than that, it appears that they are aware of the potential for regeneration of cerebral activity. Bartlett believed that this was their primary motivation in shrinking the heads of their loved ones."

"You mean...?"

The professor nodded gravely. "To prevent an accidental reboot."

"Like a computer?"

"Exactly like a computer. How often have you switched off your computer and restarted it again without any ill effects?"

"Ah yes, but oxygen starvation is anathema to the brain, is it not?"

"A popular misconception, my friend. The brain is more like a computer than most people imagine and like any computer it can be switched off and on more or less at will."

"But I thought even a few minutes of oxygen starvation would cause irreparable damage."

"Consensus thinking, Footprint. Look at Bartlett. He was pronounced brain dead several hours before we revived him."

"And his brain is undamaged?"

"Well, we can't be sure yet how much damage it has sustained. The problem is that the rest of his body had started to decay before we managed to reboot, so however healthy his brain may be, he is bound to have difficulties."

"And if the brain is damaged beyond repair?"

"This is not a concept that we entertain. As I'm sure you are aware, the regenerative powers of the human brain are legendary, so I expect that Bartlett's brain will repair itself quite naturally – given time."

"And his memory?"

"There will be some loss of memory. I believe that is unavoidable, but much of anything that is lost can be re-learnt."

"That's remarkable," said Footprint. "And how long do you think the brain can survive after death?"

"Several days, certainly. Maybe even weeks. Who knows."

"But that's incredible!"

"Yes," the professor replied, quietly. "So you see why it is important for our work to continue?"

***

As soon as Footprint was gone, Professor Gordon hurried upstairs to the Provost's office.

The Provost was a tall distinguished-looking sil-ver-haired man of indeterminate age; his short-cropped hair and upright bearing betrayed his military origins. He stood by the window in classic Provost-pose as Gor-don entered the room. Then, with impeccable timing, he whirled on his heel, strode forward and grasped the professor's hand.

"My dear Gordon. Take a seat. The man from the Pentagon is gone, I take it?"

Professor Gordon nodded.

The Provost sat down behind his massive desk. "And he met with Bartlett?"

"He saw Bartlett. I wouldn't say he *met* with him exactly."

"Good, good. And he was duly impressed, I hope?"

"I'm not sure. He certainly made copious notes."

"Good, good."

"And how is Bartlett? Making progress, I trust?"

"Slowly."

"Has he said anything yet?"

"I think he said my name."

"Yes, and what else?"

"Not much."

"And you still insist that his brain is active?"

"Yes."

"And undamaged."

"Largely, yes."

The Provost stood. He circled his desk and sat on a corner peering down at Gordon over his half-spectacles. "You are aware that I will be leaving this position soon."

"Yes, of course. I remember the announcement. You are to head up a new Foundation."

"The Society for Universal Co-operation and Knowledge."

"That's SUCK."

"Precisely. You will be aware that I have put your name forward as my replacement."

Professor Gordon had heard rumors, but he feigned surprise. "That is most generous of you, Provost."

"Before I go, Gordon, I would like to ensure the success of your project. You must be aware how highly I regard the work of your department."

"Indeed. Thank you, Provost."

"I see your work as seminal. If you are successful, the implications could be far-reaching."

"Yes, I believe so."

"Revolutionary, ground-breaking even."

"Indeed."

"This could be the greatest scientific breakthrough since Darwin."

"Oh, I don't know—"

"To put it bluntly, the legacy of my tenure as Provost of this Institute may hinge on the success of this project."

Professor Gordon swallowed hard.

The Provost continued, "So what are the chances of success?"

"There are difficulties..."

"What difficulties?"

"Well, Bartlett's brain seems fine, but I'm not sure that his other organs are up to the task, Provost. His vocal chords may be damaged, and many of his fundamental physiological functions are highly erratic. He's eating and drinking very little. His kidneys, his liver, his heart are all suspect."

"If there is anything I can do to help, you must not hesitate to ask."

"Thank you, Provost."

"Is it a question of money?" the Provost asked bluntly.

"Well, yes. I believe we can rebuild his basic physiology. But I will need two vital pieces of equipment."

"And these are?"

"A dialysis machine to circulate and cleanse the blood."

"And?"

"A hyperbaric chamber."

"And the cost?"

"Difficult to estimate. Maybe two hundred thousand dollars."

"For both?"

"Each."

The Provost never blinked. "Very well. Go ahead and acquire them immediately. And if you need more money at any stage, please let me know."

***

The dialysis machine was acquired from a local hospital and a hyperbaric chamber from the US Navy. The hospital also supplied eight pints of blood matched for Bartlett. Under the professor's guidance, Smedley and Cardew worked round the clock, and within three days they had a working heart-lung machine. The dialysis machine was used to pump the blood through the hyperbaric unit. Inside the hyperbaric unit, it flowed through an elaborate maze of tubing made of a porous substance which facilitated the transfer of oxygen into the blood under high pressure.

The next two days and nights were spent adjusting the rate of flow of the blood around the loop and fine-tuning the pressure in the hyperbaric chamber so that the oxygen uptake was just right.

Finally, the moment of truth arrived. Bartlett's head was severed from his failing body, connected to the new heart-lung machine and rebooted.

***

Weeks of intense monitoring followed, using the most sophisticated of electroencephalographs. The results were less than encouraging.

"It's hopeless, Professor."

"Be patient, Smedley. Look at the encephalograph traces. See those alpha waves? And what about those pre-frontal traces."

"Looks like non-REM sleep."

"Exactly. There's a lot of activity going on in there. Trust me."

"I dunno, professor. It's been how long?"

"We've got to allow time for the repair mechanisms to kick in. I expect the new Bartlett will be much better than the old one."

"I hope so."

"Just wait. You'll see."

***

It was nighttime when Bartlett opened his eyes. The laboratory was in darkness and he was alone. He opened his mouth, but no sound came out. He closed his mouth. Then he closed his eyes again and went back to sleep.

***

Associate professor Claude Shortsnips was head of the Department of Robotics. After four years in residence he had succeeded in duplicating a basic robotic arm from a blueprint supplied by General Motors, and one of his graduate students had developed a working ocular instrument adapted from an endoscope.

Shortsnips beamed at Professor Gordon. "You need my help?"

"So it seems," Gordon responded between clenched teeth.

"Tell me what you need."

Professor Gordon took a deep breath. "We need a speech synthesizer for a human brain."

"Bartlett's brain."

"That's right. If you can provide us with even a rudimentary speech function, that would be a huge step forward. Can you do it?"

"I may be able to. We have something in development...My budget would have to be expanded..."

"That shouldn't be a problem."

"...enormously."

"It doesn't have to be very sophisticated, Shortsnips."

"I understand. Let me think on it."

"How long will it take?"

"Difficult to say. The interface is the thing. If you can tap into the appropriate nerve centers in the brain, then I should be able to provide the required functionality."

"You have six weeks," said Professor Gordon.

"Why six weeks?"

"That's the deadline for the project's next major review."

***

Several weeks passed. The funds for the project doubled, then trebled, then doubled again. Shortsnips bought himself a new car.

Bartlett awoke from his slumber and established eye-contact with his colleagues. he seemed alert, possibly even annoyed. His brain was clearly functioning. Of course, he could say nothing, but Smedley and the professor worked out a simple system of communication based on blinking: one blink for *yes*, two blinks for *no*, three blinks for *I don't know.*

"How do you feel, Bartlett? Do you feel any pain?"

No.

"Do you know where you are?

I don't know.

"Do you know who you are?"

Yes.

"And do you know who I am?"

Yes.

"This is Smedley. Do you remember Smedley?"

Four blinks. *Yes, yes* or *I don't know, no.*

"And Cardew. You remember Cardew the postgrad?"

Yes.

Smedley acquired a small metal trolley with wheels and three shelves from the canteen. Bartlett's head was mounted in a custom-made receptacle on the top. The hyperbaric unit and the dialysis machine occupied the other two shelves and a duvet cover decorated with a large floral pattern was adapted to cover the trolley so only Bartlett's head could be seen protruding from the top.

Smedley and Cardew stood back to admire their work.

"What does he look like to you, Smedley?"

"He looks very dignified. A little short, perhaps."

The bespectacled post-grad smiled. "I think he looks like a pint-sized ambassador from some African country."

"Yes, perhaps the floral pattern is a little over the top."

"Or a miniature body builder. Those shoulders..."

"I suppose we could make him taller and less ... square. Do you like your new clothes, Bartlett?"

No answer.

By the time Shortsnips was ready for a first trial run of his speech interface, Professor Gordon and Smedley had successfully mapped out the functions of all of Bartlett's main nerve-endings, based largely on information obtained by Cardew from the Internet. Bartlett's duvet cover had been replaced by a smart woolen garment of charcoal gray with a strong pinstripe.

Shortsnips arrived late, dragging with him a small teletype machine complete with stand and a stack of continuous paper.

An argument started immediately.

"We asked for speech synthesis." Professor Gordon complained. "This is just a glorified typewriter."

"Yes, but speech synthesis was not practical. Not in the time available."

"And you are proposing what, exactly?"

"We've built an interface to the teletype. Bartlett will be able to print out his responses."

"And speech synthesis?"

"We should be able to provide that eventually, given enough time."

"How much time?"

"A couple of years, maybe."

***

Bartlett was connected to the teletype machine and the team tried to get Shortsnips's interface to work. They placed Bartlett on his trolley directly in front of the teletype to provide him with feedback. Day after day they labored with Bartlett without any success. The evenings were occupied with meetings where Professors Gordon and Shortsnips railed at one another.

"Your interface doesn't work!"

"My interface is fine. Your nerve mapping must be wrong. Or else Bartlett is simply brain dead."

Three weeks passed and the teletype produced nothing. Then, one morning when Cardew opened up the laboratory, he found a short character sequence on the teletype's paper.

tktx kstsm gmmqm

The professor was delighted. "Don't you see what this means, Cardew? Bartlett has had to *learn* how to communicate with the teletype."

"And what does his message mean?"

"It means that he has made a breakthrough. Can't you see? It won't be long now until Bartlett is communicating with us properly."

The next morning there was a whole line of unintelligible print on the teletype. The last character on the line was completely blackened, having been overprinted dozens of times.

"He needs to find the carriage return and linefeed characters," said the professor.

The morning after that there was nothing, but at lunchtime the day after that the teletype chattered into action and a page and a half of characters poured out.

The professor was ecstatic. "He's got the hang of the carriage return and linefeed characters."

"But it's nothing but gibberish," Smedley sighed.

"Yes, but it's readable gibberish."

At lunchtime the day after that, the teletype chattered into action. All day it continued, filling page after page with apparently random characters. By the evening, they had to switch off the teletype to replace the ribbon, and when they switched it on again the stream of output resumed almost immediately.

After twenty-four hours and two more ribbon changes, they had to switch the teletype off, as it was starting to smoke gently.

All three men took turns examining the mountainous printout, but it was nonsensical.

Cardew put the kettle on.

"I think we must assume the worst," Smedley murmured.

The professor raised an eyebrow. "And that is?"

"Bartlett is insane."

"Nonsense!"

"I agree with Smedley," Cardew said, dropping four teabags into the kettle.

"And what about the carriage return and linefeed?" demanded the professor.

Smedley shrugged his huge shoulders and Cardew poured out three cups of strong tea.

***

By the time General Alpenstock arrived to review the work of the project, the Provost had taken up his new position as head of SUCK and Professor Gordon had been designated 'Acting Provost', pending his official appointment.

The teletype was switched on and the professor said: "Bartlett, this is General Alpenstock. He is here to meet you."

The teletype chattered: w*wep hodtrr*

The general put his face close to Bartlett's. "Hello Bartlett. How are you?"

zzzq2 replied the teletype.

"Is that the best he can do?" The general asked the Acting Provost.

"We're working on it, General."

General Alpenstock peered into Bartlett's eyes.

"He seems alert. Is this conveyance really necessary?" He indicated the trolley.

"Yes, General. Without it Bartlett's brain would be starved of oxygen and he could not function."

"So how mobile is he?"

"We can push him around the laboratory."

"He can't move about on his own?"

"No."

The general snorted. "Quite a severe limiting factor, wouldn't you say, Gordon?"

"Yes, General, but I'm sure we could provide him with independent mobility if that were a priority."

"It is. And fix him up with an arm."

"An arm."

"So that he can salute."

"Right, General. Anything else?"

"You could make him taller. If we decide to draft him into the Armed Forces, he will need to be able to look the other men in the eye."

"Yes, sir."

***

Smedley and Cardew went to work immediately, adding two feet of aluminum tubing to make Bartlett taller. They engineered servos to drive the trolley wheels and adapted a wheelchair circuit so that Bartlett could steer by moving his eyes. Then they removed the teletype from its stand and incorporated it onto Bartlett's trolley.

Acting Provost Gordon paid a visit to the robotics department and asked Shortsnips to build a new interface to enable Bartlett to operate the General Motors robot arm.

"My budget, Acting Provost—"

"Yes, I know," Gordon replied.

***

While Bartlett's efforts at communications continued a failure, his skills with the wheelchair controls were soon apparent. Cardew survived a couple of near misses when Bartlett drove at him at speed. Smedley, on the other hand, was not so lucky. He had difficulty moving his massive bulk out of the way in time and suffered a number of painful injuries to his lower limbs.

Bartlett's wheels were silent, the sound of the servos almost inaudible, allowing him to glide around the laboratory with barely a sound. He would feign sleep in the morning, and then sneak up behind them when their backs were turned. He seemed to delight in such childish pranks and, while the expression on his face could never have been mistaken for a smile, there may have been a twinkle in his eyes.

***

The day that Shortsnips arrived with the robotic arm marked a major turning point for the project. The interface worked first time, and Bartlett rushed about the laboratory lashing out with his new limb at everything and anything he could reach. Within ten minutes, every surface in the laboratory had been swept clear, the floor was covered with papers, broken glass and crockery and Smedley had a black eye.

"Ouch!" Smedley waved a fist at Bartlett. "That hurt."

"Leave Bartlett alone," said the professor. "Go wait outside."

Smedley lumbered off, muttering to himself.

"Cardew," the professor said, "I'm handing the project over to you for a while. Bartlett will need to learn how to control the arm, and you are just the man to teach him."

"Seems he has a fair idea how to use it already," Cardew said, surveying the destruction.

"He will need to develop fine-motor skills, so that he can use the fingers. See what you can achieve in a week."

***

A week later, the professor entered the laboratory. Smedley adjusted his shin-guards and followed him in.

They found Cardew and Bartlett playing checkers. The professor watched, fascinated, as Bartlett reached his robotic arm across the board and pushed one of his pieces forward.

The professor beamed. "I see you've made some great progress, Cardew."

Cardew nodded without taking his eyes from the game. "His checkers is improving by leaps and bounds. I reckon he's already too good for me."

"His fine-motor control is amazing. Teaching him to play checkers is a bonus."

Cardew looked up from the board. "It wasn't difficult. Once he grasped the basic moves, he picked it up right away."

"He may have a residual memory of the game," Smedley said.

Bartlett raised his robotic arm, pointed it in Smedley's direction and gave him the finger.

Smedley squeaked.

"Very impressive," said the professor.

***

A couple of mornings later, they discovered a short message on the teletype page. It read:

thou shal not kil

Smedley tore it off and handed it to the professor. "His spelling's not up to much," he said. "And shouldn't that be 'shalt'?"

"Never mind his spelling," said the professor. "His communications interface is working at last."

He dashed over to Bartlett and asked him a question. "Bartlett, do you know who I am?"

Bartlett opened his eyes. His robotic arm rose into the air, hovered over the teletype keyboard, extended a finger, and typed:

gordno

"That's right," said the professor. "And what is your name?"

barlet

"This is amazing," the professor said. "He's using the robotic arm to type out his answers. I always knew Shortsnips's neural interface for the teletype was a crock of shit."

"We don't need it now," Cardew said.

"That's right. Bartlett can type his answers."

Bartlett's robotic fingers were drumming on the trolley. Then his arm moved again. It typed:

wy am i

"What does that mean?" Smedley said.

"I think he wants us to explain his continuing existence," Cardew said.

"Do you remember what happened to you?" the professor said.

Bartlett made no response.

"You had an accident in the Natural History hall. Don't you remember?"

Still no response.

"The narwhal skeleton fell on you. You were impaled on its horn."

Nothing.

"Maybe he doesn't remember. It all happened very suddenly," Smedley said.

"What is the last thing you remember?" Professor Gordon said.

why anm i

"This is getting us nowhere," Smedley said. "Put the kettle on, Cardew."

***

General Alpenstock's eyes lit up when he saw the teletype printouts. "Looks like there really is something going on in there."

"Oh he's very intelligent," Smedley said. "Tell him Cardew."

Cardew nodded. "He plays a mean game of checkers, and I've been teaching him to play chess."

"He doesn't need to be a genius," the general said. "We're looking for a footsoldier with just enough brainpower to obey orders without question. Get him to type something for me."

"Bartlett. Tell the general how you're feeling today," the professor said.

The fingers drummed, but the arm remained motionless.

Cardew stepped forward. "Bartlett, what is your name?" he said.

The robotic arm swung into action and produced:

bartelt

The professor tore off the sheet and handed it to the general.

"My, my," said the general. "This is really something. Ask him something else."

"Do you know who this is?" Cardew said, pointing to the general.

usaarmy

"Right," said the general. "Time to place this project under military control. Lock everything down, Professor. My men will be here at reveille tomorrow to relocate the project to a military installation."

The professor drew himself up to his full five foot seven. "Now hold on just a minute, General. This is my project. You can't just waltz in and take it away from me."

"I think you'll find that I can," the general replied. "Where d'you think your funding has been coming from for the past year?"

"But the project will fail without my input. No one else understands the science behind it."

"So what would you suggest?"

"Let me continue to run with it. For a while, at least."

General Alpenstock fished a cigar from his breast pocket, bit the end off, spat it out and stuck it between his lips. "Light me," he said.

Cardew produced a lighter and the general lit up. "How easily could you relocate?" he said.

"Not a problem," the professor said.

"Okay. In that case, you can stick with the project. I'll give you three months to train my team so that they can run with it. After that you'll be free to come back here and resume your academic career. Agreed?"

"Agreed."

The two men shook hands.

Bartlett blinked.

***

Smedley and Cardew sat in the empty canteen, drinking machine coffee.

Something had been troubling Cardew all afternoon. "I really don't understand what the military want with him," he said.

"We've had this discussion before, Cardew. Think how much easier it will be to recruit men to the Armed Forces when the government can show that they can cheat death, that a dead soldier can be brought back to life. Bartlett is living proof of what can be done."

"With his head on a trolley, using a robotic arm to type on an old teletype?"

"The trolley's just the first step, Cardew. Use your imagination. Shortsnips and his boys should be able to come up with a whole new artificial body."

"Which the Army will enhance."

"Enhance? How?"

"Use your imagination, Smedley."

The coffee tasted foul.

***

Cardew broke into the laboratory at three in the morning. Bartlett was wide awake. Cardew set up the checkers on the board.

"Fancy a game, old friend?" he said.

ches not checkers

Cardew replaced the checkers with chess pieces. He made a move. Bartlett replied. After fourteen moves, Cardew was in trouble. He had brought his queen out too early, and Bartlett had her trapped.

"We need to talk."

about

"About the future. You heard what the general said?"

he will move me

Cardew nodded. "To a secret military installation somewhere."

i will be soldier

"Yes. How do you feel about that?"

There was a long pause before Bartlett replied.

shold be dead

"Yes, but Professor Gordon brought you back to life."

i shuld be dead

"Do you want to be a soldier?"

no

"The military will give you a new body. You'll be able to leave this trolley, walk again."

Bartlett gave that some thought before responding:

like i was

"No. I think they'll give you an artificial body with armor-plating. You'll be enhanced for war."

There was another very long pause before Bartlett's arm moved to the keyboard again.

they wil use m to make army

"Yes, I think they will."

end it

Cardew looked into Bartlett's eyes. There were no tears, but Cardew sensed an immense weariness there. "You wish to die?"

end me

***

The fire was like nothing the academics had ever seen. The heat was intense. Flames shot forty feet into the air, and there was a series of explosions as the chemical contents of the laboratory ignited. In an attempt to salvage his life's work, Professor Gordon rushed in and was consumed by the inferno.

Sifting through the debris after the fire had burnt itself out, the soldiers found no trace of Bartlett, apart from the twisted remains of a robotic arm.

***

They gave Smedley Professor Gordon's job. Cardew left the university to start as a management trainee with Wal-mart. Shortsnips got to be Provost.

POPPING THE QUESTION

I WISH YOU LUCK, mate. No hard feelings. No. We broke up a couple or three months ago.

You've noticed there's something about her? It's not just the way she holds herself, the angle of her head, her gait, her long stride or the strange spring in her step. It's not her odd laugh and the way it erupts for no reason.

You're right. It's something else.

Yes, her eyes are probably unique. Have you noticed how far apart they are? And what about the color! Have you seen eyes that color on anyone else? Me neither. And then there's her hair, of course. Everyone thinks it's dyed, but it's not, that's it's natural color.

Have you seen her naked? No? Well you're in for a treat, mate. I've never seen such a beautiful figure, her flawless back rising to an impossibly long neck. I often used to wonder if I took the trouble to count her vertebrae would I find that she had more than she should have. I never did. Perhaps I was afraid of what I might discover.

Give her my regards. No, honestly I have no regrets. Water under the bridge, ancient history and all that.

Oh, by the way, watch out for her fingers. She always had long, thin fingers, but these days they're like needles topped with nails filed to points. Don't say I didn't warn you.

No, why should I be jealous? I told you: we're no longer an item, and even when we were dating regularly she was seeing other men. She never made a secret of it, and I didn't object. The way I looked at it, there was just too much woman there to be satisfied by one man.

We broke up in the summer.

We'd been swimming. I caught a glimpse of the soles of her feet. They were covered in green scales. No, that wasn't why. It was later that day. We were watching the sun go down. I was playing my guitar. I sang a few songs – you know.

Yes, it was romantic. But then, out of the blue, she popped the question.

That was the deal-breaker for me. I walked away.

The question?

She said, "How long have you lived among humans?"

SHORT BACK AND SIDES

Next, please.

Good afternoon, sir. And what would you like? Just a tidy up? Of course. And how would you like it? Short or long at the back? A good bit off the top? Short back and sides, perhaps? I beg your pardon? Go easy on the fringe? Yes, sir.

Just slip your arms in here sir. That's it.

My, it has been a while, hasn't it, sir? Been away have we? Oh yes, on holidays. Anywhere exotic? Somewhere windy perhaps. I beg your pardon? Atlanta. In Georgia. Yes I know where it is. Are you sure it wasn't Chicago? Chicago, Illinois. You know, the windy city. Never mind, sir. Just my quirky sense of humour.

If you wouldn't mind just holding your head up a bit, sir. That's fine.

I had a funny week, last week, sir. On Monday, I moved into a new flat. My mother wasn't too happy about it, I can tell you but, well, you can't live with your mother forever, can you? And quite frankly, we have started getting on one another's nerves. The new flat is a mess, but I have plans to redecorate and once I start to put some pieces of furniture in, I'll soon beat it into shape. Hmm? Oh, not too far from here. It's handy enough for work. Just a short bus journey.

You've a fine head of hair, sir. Very thick at the back. What? Oh, no fear of that sir, none at all. You'll take your hair with you to your grave. Chin up, please sir. Thank you.

It has just one bedroom, but that's plenty, don't you think? A small kitchen - a kitchenette, the landlord calls it, and a reasonable living room. I expect I'll be very happy there.

On Tuesday, I was ill. I found some cheese in the fridge in the new flat. It looked okay, so I decided to chance it. I didn't have very much of it, but boy was I sick. Up most of the night with stomach cramps.

Head back, please sir. A little to the left. Thank you.

Wednesday was wet. You remember how wet it was, sir. Bucketing down it was all day. I got soaked just standing at the bus stop in the morning, and then I got soaked again on the way home in the evening.

Thursday, I was abducted by aliens.

Nigel. Put him down, Nigel.

Excuse me a moment, sir.

Nigel, a word in your ear, please. I don't think you should manhandle the customers like that. Not even the small ones. Nigel, did you hear me? Put that child down. Yes, I know it's difficult to keep your mind on your work, with all that running about going on. Yes, all right, Nigel, I'll have a word with her and see what I can do. Put him down, Nigel. I've said. I will talk to the customer, but you must put the child down.

Madam, I must ask you to please control your off-spring. They are upsetting Nigel. Yes I can see they are only children, but they are disturbing the staff. If you wouldn't mind just keeping them under control. Thank you, Madam.

Sorry about that, sir. Poor Nigel, he's not the brightest. He's a wonderful hairdresser, of course. An artist with a brush and scissors, but he's easily distracted. And his health is not the best. It's his veins. He suffers terribly with his varicose veins. He'd be much better off if he wasn't on his feet all day long. And I've told him, so on numerous occasions.

Head forward, sir. Thank you.

Where was I? Oh yes, Thursday. I was abducted by aliens. Yes, sir. Extraterrestrials. From another planet. I don't know which planet, just not this one.

No, I tell a lie. It was Friday. I remember it was Friday because I took my mother to the homeopathy clinic on Thursday and I collected my new jacket from the shop on the way home. And after supper I went to my dancing class. Very good exercise is dancing. You should try it, sir. Not that I mean to suggest that you're overweight, not at all, sir. In fact I would say you have a very trim figure. Very Brad Pitt if I may say so.

You work out? Well, I'm not surprised, sir. And it looks well on you too, sir.

Anyway, I was on my way home on Friday. To my new flat - on the bus, yes, sir - when all of a sudden there was this strange eerie light. Sort of bluish and very bright. It seemed to be coming from everywhere. The bus shook and I found myself floating up out of my seat. I passed right through the roof of the bus. No sir, I never felt a thing. One minute I was sitting in my seat, next minute I was floating above the roof of the bus surrounded in this strange blue light.

I must have passed out, because when I awoke I was lying on a table, with lots of lights and instruments, like dentists' drills. My wrists and ankles were strapped down and there were aliens peering at me from all sides.

Imagine my surprise when I realized that I had nothing on. No, sir, not a stitch. Stark naked, as the day I was born. The only thing I could think of was what had happened to my new leather jacket. It was sort of double breasted with deep lapels, very butch zips and lots of steel studs. Very Schwarzenegger. Did you see *Terminator*, sir? The film, sir. It had Arnold Schwarzenegger on a motorcycle. Nevermind, sir.

The aliens? Ugly little creatures. You've seen the photos, I expect. Big buggy eyes and spindly legs and arms. Gives me goose pimples all over just thinking about them.

Hmm? Oh, I'd rather not go into the gruesome details, sir, but just let me say that it was not nice. Quite upsetting, in fact.

The next time I awoke I was in a small metal room. I was dressed in some sort of smock, a bit like a hospital gown.

What was it like? Very plain. No pattern at all, but the material was quite unusual. Sort of shiny and smooth with no joins or seams anywhere.... Oh, the room. The walls were metal, and the room was roughly cylindrical. There was some light, but I couldn't tell where it was coming from. It was obvious that I was on a spaceship and I could tell from the thrum, thrum of the engines that we were heading into outer space.

Thrum, thrum. Yes, sir.

Would you like it off the ears or on the ears, sir? Off? Yes, perhaps you're right. Head to the side please, sir. Thank you.

Anyway, after about two weeks, we arrived at their planet. Yes, sir. I know. Well it felt like two weeks, all right? Yes, sir. This all happened last Friday. Yes, sir. That's right, sir. Do you want me to tell you this story or not? Okay.

Chin up just a bit. That's lovely.

The aliens' planet was barren and desolate. No vegetation anywhere, just the remains of large metal buildings, like skyscrapers. Like cylindrical metal skyscrapers, everywhere you looked. The sky was a deep crimson. Not like our sunsets. This was a sinister, threatening sky.

I beg your pardon? Yes, yes. It was a typical saucer-shaped craft. About the size of a small city, say Phoenix Arizona or Las Vegas. We were led down the gangplank and taken to one of the metal buildings. Oh, did I mention the others? There were six of us - three men and three women.

After arriving in the metal building, we were spoken to by the aliens. When I say spoken to.... they communicated with us but not through sounds. It was as if they spoke directly to our minds. English? No. It was a form of communication beyond language. No, not like pictures. More like ideas.

They told us of their great war. It seems there were just two great powers on their planet, like our superpowers, I suppose. Two great nations that each wanted to rule the whole planet. There was a battle of words. Neither nation was prepared to back down and both were equipped for war. And so of course it happened. First, there were small border skirmishes, then there were major incursions and localized battles, and before long the whole planet was at war.

This was a war unlike anything on Earth. Total war with only one outcome - the complete destruction of their civilization. The war lasted for a long long time, maybe three hundred of our years. Generation after generation of aliens were born and died and still the war continued. Finally, the warring factions turned to biological weapons, and the whole species began to die. You had to feel sorry for them, poor ugly little bug eyed aliens.

Other side, sir. Thank you.

Their technology is far superior to ours, of course, and this gave them their one great hope for the future of their world: space-time travel. They had been watching us on Earth for many centuries and conducting experiments to see if there was a way to save their species. They considered colonizing Earth, but their gene pool had been contaminated, their birth rate had fallen to zero. Their scientists tried to harvest our DNA, to find a way to regenerate their own by transplanting some of ours, but the differences were too great. Their DNA has been evolving for millions of years longer than ours, you see, sir. I suppose mixing our DNA with theirs would be like adding muddy water to Starbucks coffee.

Anyway, when all their experiments failed, they sent one of their few remaining intergalactic spaceships to travel to Earth and bring back some human specimens to re-populate their planet. I suppose they decided that if they couldn't maintain their own species, and they couldn't interbreed with us, then they would rather pass their planet on to a new human population than to have their whole culture and civilization die with them.

Now, there you are, sir. How's that? How about the fringe? Is that okay for you? Would you like a little spray?

No spray? Here you are sir, use this brush. Pay on the way out. Don't leave it so long next time.

My new leather jacket? Gone, sir. I never saw it again. I expect some bug-eyed alien is wearing it in now, in some far away galaxy.

The others? Funny thing, sir, but I knew the other two men. One of them is a regular at our dancing troupe. We meet on Thursday nights. He has the most divine passe doble. The other guy is a friend of a friend. He runs a small tattoo parlor down by the docks and is a bit of a cross dresser.

The women? No, I didn't know any of the women, sir.

Goodbye, sir. Oh, thank you very much, sir. Have a nice day.

Next, please.

OOZE

THE EMPRESS WAS MORE viscous than many of her subjects. Her mucosity was legendary, her slime admired everywhere she slithered. At little over 200,000 years old, many considered her too young for high office. Some thought she curried favor too greasily, others that she spread herself too thin. And yet her royal ooziness was well liked by the young-saps.

The Empress's latest offspring, eVVe, "the strange" was aptly named. She was a loner, spending much of her time separated from the Mass in muddy pools, cavorting in mountain streams or pouring over waterfalls, mixing with all manner of shameless semi-liquids. eVVe exulted in her oily liquefaction and her thoughts often diverged from the norm. The Empress despaired at the depth of eVVe's individuality. And, as is always the way, the sniggering Mass took secret pleasure in her royal ooziness's misfortune.

Life on planet QaaQ was lubricious. There was always light and abundant heat; the two suns, S1 and her daughter, S2, filling the sky, turn and turn about.

For 112,000 years, QaaQ had orbited S2 but the time had come when S1's gravity would seize QaaQ and the planet would transition to an orbit of the larger sun. The Blessed Unction had arrived.

The ground shook. All over QaaQ volcanoes grumbled; some erupted, and the sky grew grainier with each successive rotation. The population rippled in ever-increasing excitement, for the transition from one sun to the other was the most revered event in the QaaQ calendar. Some of the more extreme eruptions gave rise to concern among the younger generation—eVVe, for one, had the feeling that the planet was tearing itself apart—but for the older Mass members, the Blessed Unction was nothing to be feared. The frequent seismic events were especially welcome, as they disturbed the crawlers, shaking them from their hiding places in the rock crevices.

***

The Galactic Explorer, GE Millington, slipped into an uneasy outer orbit around the binary pair and began detailed charting and a spectroscopic survey of the system. Seventy-three planets were identified as well as countless planetoids and asteroids. Seventy-two of the planets orbited beyond the rotational domain of the binary pair. The remaining planet, designated MMG73, occupied a curious, unstable position between the two suns. This planet orbited the white dwarf, but it was clear from the pattern of its orbit that it would soon switch to an orbit of the much larger red giant. Of the seventy three planets, only MMG73 had an atmosphere. It also had an abundance of water, but it seemed unlikely that it could support life, as it was seething with active volcanoes resulting from the extreme gravitational stresses exerted by the two suns.

***

The first rotation of the Blessed Unction began. To the voiceless cheers of the common mucous, the Keeper of the Sacred Phlegm – whose name was unpronounceable – slithered to the foot of the mountain and began her glutinous ascent. As the small bright sun, S2, slid behind her mother, S1, the entire lubricant population of the planet took their places. Silently, their bodies formed an unbroken oleaginous chain all around the base of the mountain. Even eVVe abandoned her watery pursuits and joined the Mass. A quiver ran through her body as she absorbed a passing ~mmmmmmg crawler.

Mass-mind was unaware of color, the extreme luminosity of both suns having limited QaaQi evolution to monochromatic eyes, but they were aware that the small sun was hot, the large sun hotter. Reproduction was only possible while S2 was in the ascendancy. As long as S1 was mistress of the sky, QaaQ would be a sultry, sybaritic paradise, the sweltering population too soporific to do anything other than simmer in the perpetual inferno, feasting on the planet's crawlers.

***

Crewman Pauli flushed with pride. He knew it was unprofessional, but he couldn't help it. It happened every time one of his predictions proved accurate and this latest one was a doozy!

He found Supervisor Coetzee in the recreation area playing Go with Captain Dennison. The game was nearly over; supervisor Coetzee's white pieces controlled more than half the board; it was only a matter of time before the captain's black pieces were surrounded and wiped out.

Pauli sat at the bar and watched the game grind its way toward the inevitable end. He groaned inwardly. Why couldn't the captain admit defeat? His situation was hopeless.

"Stop that, Crewman," Captain Dennison said, without taking his eyes from the board.

"Stop what?"

"Tapping your fingers on the counter."

Pauli snorted petulantly and wandered off to the other end of the bar. He ordered a small fermented fruit drink.

When the captain finally conceded, Supervisor Coetzee joined Pauli at the bar. The crewman tried to break the news as casually as he could.

"It's happening," he said.

"What is?"

"MMG73's orbital switch."

"That's what you expected, isn't it?"

"Yes. And it started right on time."

"Fine, so where's the problem?"

"There's no problem. I just thought you might be interested, is all."

"Don't bother me with trivialities, Pauli. Keep a weather eye on it and give me a heads-up if anything unexpected happens, okay?"

"Okay."

"How about a quick game?"

***

Halfway up the mountain, the Keeper of the Sacred Phlegm reached out and established concourse with the multitude. When she had Mass-mind's undivided attention, she raised her thoughts in prayer.

"Small mother S2, we thank you for watching over us while your mother was away wandering the heavens. We thank you for blessing us with healthy offspring and we wish you well on your journey."

"Thank you small mother," the multitude murmured voicelessly.

"Giant Mother S1! Holy slime! Into our lives once more we welcome you. Patiently have we waited for Your Glorious Unctuousness to grace our lives. Lubricate us. Embrocate us with your oily balm. Wax us with your viscid unguents, help us extrude the grit from our souls, and shake the crawlers from their hiding places."

"Amen," the multitude intoned silently.

As if in answer to the prayer, the planet lurched, the ground shuddered and two giant volcanoes exploded, punctuating the rumbles of the earth. Sulfurous ash filled the sky, and rocks and pumice rained down. In the distance several giant lava flows spread iridescent and the temperature rose. As one, the multitude swayed and rippled to the rhythm of the ground tremors. Disturbed by the seismic activity, great throngs of crawlers emerged onto the surface, only to be snaffled up by the Mass, their nutrients extracted, absorbed and shared by all.

Within one short rotation, volcanic ask filled the sky, obscuring both suns. The temperature continued to rise.

Twenty rotations passed before the sky began to clear and the suns could be seen again. Some thought that S1 looked larger; others scoffed, but all were agreed that S2 was noticeable smaller and higher in the sky.

And so the Blessed Unction progressed, rotation by rotation, until S1 filled the sky and S2 was like a small, bright, distant moon. The Keeper of the Sacred Phlegm knew that, within a few rotations, the tiny form of S2 would be absorbed by her mother. There would be universal shock and sadness at S2's passing. Seventy rotations later—if the Sacred Covenant was fulfilled—S1 would give birth to a new tiny sun, emerging fully-formed from the edge of her mother in the southern sky. And there would be great jubilation in the Mass.

***

When the small shuttle landed, it went largely unnoticed. Apart from its shape, which was smooth and symmetrical, there was little to distinguish it from the thousands of fiery boulders emitted by the volcanoes and raining down on all sides. Of all the Mass, only eVVe's suspicions were aroused when she observed the object's descent. Unlike boulders from the volcanoes falling under the force of gravity, this one had landed gently on a flat outcrop of rock.

***

Captain Dennison put away his *Readers Digest* and surveyed the scene through a tiny window.

"What d'you think, Skipper?" said Pauli, his crewman.

"Looks even more like Hell up close," said Dennison. "What's the surface temperature like out there?"

"Touching a hundred forty degrees, sir."

"Gravity?"

"Tolerable. Maybe G plus five percent."

"And the atmosphere?"

"Oxygen-nitrogen, but with heavy concentrations of sulfur dioxide and fine-grain ash."

The captain's eyes glazed over. "Fire and brimstone, in other words."

Crewman Pauli said nothing. He knew better than to disturb the captain during one of his Milton moments.

The rain came. A deluge. Hammering on the outer skin of the shuttle, it sounded like a thousand million crazed aliens desperate to smash their way in. The downpour lasted ten minutes and then stopped abruptly.

Pauli peered out the window. "I think it's stopped," he said.

"D'you think the air's breathable?"

"I doubt it, sir."

Captain Dennison sighed. "Only one way to find out. Break out the haz suits and fetch Rembrandt. The quicker we get the job done and blast off this hell-hole the better."

***

The two men emerged from the shuttle in their silver haz suits, Pauli carrying a white rat in a cage. The planet steamed like a giant sauna.

Within thirty seconds Rembrandt was twitching violently. One minute later the rat turned up its toes and died.

Through the mist the two men could see a vast yellow plain stretching out below them, surrounded by dark mountains. The sky was dark, partly obscured by a dirty cloud of super-fine volcanic ash, and dominated by the larger of the two suns. A red giant, this sun appeared purple, while its smaller companion looked like a bright blue moon sitting on its shoulder. Of course the large sun was not really purple, any more than the small one was blue. The dust particles in the upper atmosphere accounted for their strange color, and for the color of the sky itself.

"Weird," Pauli muttered.

"What, the brown clouds?" said Dennison.

"Yeah, that and the two suns, and the yellow snow. Everything, really."

"I don't think that's snow, Crewman. Not at these temperatures."

"Right. So what is it, Skipper?"

"I don't know. Let's take a closer look."

They scrambled down the slope, past steaming fissures and yellow sulfur deposits, to the edge of the plain. Up close, it looked like a vast lake stretching to the mountain.

"Looks like my mother's carrot and coriander soup," Pauli said.

Dennison shook his head inside his haz helmet. "I don't think it's liquid. It's not moving. No waves. And look closely at the edge."

Pauli hunkered down. Right where the yellow substance began there was a distinct edge, and it had thickness—maybe three millimeters. The captain was right. It wasn't liquid. Pauli poked it with a gloved finger, starting a tiny ripple that radiated away across the lake, growing as it went.

Captain Dennison pointed his Gismo—General Instrumental Scientific Monitor—at the yellow mass. "No readings," he said. "None that make any sense, anyhow."

"How's the Geiger count?" Pauli said.

Dennison checked his Gismo again. "The reading's high, but I figure that's to be expected, given the volcanic activity."

"Any life signs?"

"None."

"Strange," said Pauli. "There's no shortage of water."

Dennison said, "At these temperatures, there must be a rapid evaporation-precipitation cycle."

"You mean it's gonna rain again soon?"

"Bet your house on it.," said Dennison. "What's surprising is that it hasn't vented out of the atmosphere eons ago."

The rain started again, right on cue. Dennison's backpack fizzled in the torrent.

"What about the minerals?" Pauli shouted. "Where should we look?" Long distance spectrometry had identified the MMG binary system as a probable source of a variety of useful minerals. The detailed spectroscopic survey had pinpointed MMG73 as the exact location of many.

"Difficult to tell. Everything around here's pumice. Find me a rock sample."

Pauli hunted around until he found a heavy rock. He chipped a small piece off and zapped it with an electrolytic charge from the Gismo, then peered at the reading. "It's showing fifty percent silica, with some iron and magnesium."

"Classic mafic igneous rock," Dennison said. "Take a look over there." He pointed toward the nearest mountain.

"What am I looking at?"

"See the way the yellow stuff's laying on the slope?"

Pauli saw it. It looked as though it had washed up the contour of the mountain and stuck there, like a thin coat of paint.

The rain stopped again and the landscape immediately began to steam.

"Looks like paint," Pauli said. An involuntary shiver ran down his back.

"Don't be abstruse," Dennison said, giving his word-power word-of-the-day an airing.

A mighty seismic tremor shook the ground under their feet. Instinctively, they reached out to each other for support. Pauli dropped the Gismo.

"*Shit!*" said Dennison.

The device ricocheted off the rock and sailed out over the lake. When it hit the surface it bounced, then rolled, coming to rest fifty feet out.

"Oops!" Pauli said. Then, "It floats!"

"Shit!" said Dennison again.

A creature like a four-foot long, segmented millipede leapt from a steaming fissure and scuttled over Pauli's boot.

"Holy crap!" he shouted, instinctively kicking out at the creature, propelling it onto the lake. The millipede landed on its back, righted itself immediately, and headed back toward the shore as fast as its legs would go. It had traveled no more than a couple of yards before a small wave rose from the lake's surface and folded itself over the creature. A moment later the wave disappeared and the creature was gone.

"Did you see that, Skipper?" Pauli said.

"I'm not sure what I saw." Dennison's voice sounded strained.

"The yellow paint stuff swallowed the creepy-crawler creature."

"Right. That's what I thought I saw. Let's get on with it."

Pauli said, "I'll get the Gismo, Skipper," taking a step toward the lake.

Dennison held out a restraining arm. "Not so fast, Crewman. We don't know that it'll support your weight."

Captain Dennison picked up Pauli's rock and threw it. It bounced and rolled to a halt. Concentric ripples ran across the surface, radiating outward from the rock and running on and on eerily to the horizon on all sides, apparently without diminution.

Pauli said, "Looks strong enough."

"Okay, I'll go," said Captain Dennison.

He pulled a rope from Pauli's backpack. Pauli tied one end around the captain's waist and wrapped the other end around his own shoulders. Captain Dennison placed a foot on the yellow lake and tested it. It held firm. Taking a deep breath, he put both feet on the surface. It wobbled like rubber, but supported his weight well enough. He took a few steps away from the edge, stopped, and flexed his knees. The surface reacted like a trampoline, but with a strange dampened effect and more weird ripples.

With each step, volcanic ash fell from Captain Dennison's boots, leaving dark footprints on the surface.

Dennison was twelve feet from the Gismo when Pauli called out, "Don't you think that's odd, Skipper?"

"What? Don't be abstruse, Crewman."

"Look at your footprints, sir. And why are there no boulders on the surface?"

"What d'you mean? There's one."

"Yes, but shouldn't there be more? And shouldn't there be a layer of ash on there, given the active volcanoes?"

Pauli was spooked. He wondered if the captain was too.

Dennison hesitated. "I expect the rain washed it all away," he said with a wave of his gloved hand.

Three rapid steps took him to the Gismo. He picked it up and turned back. That was when Pauli knew the captain was spooked; his face was white as a ghost behind the visor of his helmet.

Dennison's boots began to sink.

"You're sinking, Skipper!" Pauli shouted, taking up the slack in the rope.

"I can see that, Crewman," Dennison said. "Give me some help. Use the rope."

Pauli pulled on the rope and Dennison managed two steps, sinking further each time. Another short half-step and Dennison came to a halt, buried to his knees in yellow goo. He was no more than twelve yards from safety.

"It's slimy underneath. I can't get any purchase," he said. "Pull harder, Crewman."

Pauli wrapped the rope around his waist and applied his full weight to the task, the prospect of losing his skipper in this desolate hell too horrible to contemplate. He had no success. With so much loose pumice on the ground, it was impossible to find a firm footing. Dennison sank as far as his hips. Leaning forward, he dug his fingers into the rubbery material in an attempt to drag himself free. Pauli continued to heave on the rope, but it was hopeless.

Pauli dropped the rope and stepped out onto the lake.

"Stay back," Dennison shouted. "That's an order."

Pauli ignored him. "Take my hands, Skipper."

Dennison dropped the Gismo and they locked arms. Pauli pulled as hard as he could, but Captain Dennison remained stuck fast.

The lake began to wave and fold over Pauli's boots. Panicked, he tugged at them and managed a couple of backward steps before he, too, became bogged down in the rubbery slime.

In desperation Pauli pulled out his sidearm and fired into the lake. The bullet vanished below the surface with a soft *schplock* sound. *Schplock, schplock, schplock, schplock, schplock, schplock, schplock, schplock, schplock.* Pauli emptied his gun into the yellow rubber.

Both men continued to sink.

"Any ideas, Skipper?" Pauli said.

Dennison shook his head. The horror in his eyes told Pauli everything: The captain was resigned to his fate. The glutinous yellow material had reached Dennison's chest. It was over Pauli's knees already.

"If they come looking for us they'll find the Gismo. That should warn them to stay clear," Dennison said. "You've been a great crewman, Crewman. It was an honor to serve with you."

"You too, sir."

"Aren't you afraid?" Dennison said.

"No sir. Not yet, anyway." Pauli's mother had always said he lacked imagination.

As if someone had turned on a faucet, the rain came again. The torrent bounced on the surface of the lake and ran off on all sides in rivulets. Like a thousand million tiny aliens clawing at their haz suits, it pounded on the two men, forcing them deeper into the yellow goo.

Dennison's backpack fizzled and sparked.

"The battery in your backpack's shorting out," Pauli shouted above the din.

The backpack fizzled again and flashed.

The lake shuddered. Wrinkles appeared on the surface. Then two big waves formed on either side of the captain and, with a slow slurping sound, he was ejected onto the surface like a cork from a bottle. Picking up the Gismo, Dennison stumbled to the safety of the rocky shore.

The rain stopped. Two beats later and the whole scene misted up as the water began to evaporate again.

Dennison set his Gismo for mineral analysis and fired a short burst of electrolytic charge close to Pauli's boots. Pauli was ejected from the lake, and Dennison helped him ashore.

Sitting side by side at the edge of the lake, the two men took a few minutes to get their breath back. Then Dennison said, "We should take a sample."

"Right, Skipper," said Pauli. "And then can we get outta here?"

"You bet!"

Pauli took a small sample jar and a sharp knife from his fanny sack. Crouching at the edge of the lake, he lowered the knife toward the yellow material.

The edge of the lake shrank back six inches.

"Holy crap!" Pauli said. "Did you see that, Skipper?"

"No. What?" Dennison looked up from checking the damage to his backpack.

"It saw the knife coming and... and..."

"What're you saying, Crewman?"

Pauli shook his head. "I'm not sure what happened, Skipper. It was like it saw the blade coming and moved outta the way." He'd survived the third battle of Pegasus IV and completed a five month rotation in the molten mines of Luciflex, but this place gave him the creeps.

"Show me," said Dennison. "Do it again."

With a slight tremor in his hands, Pauli tried again, and again the surface of the lake backed away from his blade.

"I see what you mean, Crewman," the captain said. "I think it's time we got our asses outta here."

***

eVVe's suspicions had been confirmed when the rock split open and two silver crawlers emerged. She tried to discuss the matter with her siblings, but they refused to be distracted from the religious rites, so eVVe took the problem to her mother. The Empress watched the new crawlers for a while without gaining any understanding of their actions. Unlike the native crawlers, who spent almost all their time in pursuit of g g g, these visitors seemed to eat nothing. This was more than unusual. The Empress was puzzled. How could such a big crawler support its large body-mass without spending all of its time searching for food?

The Empress reckoned they would make a fine food source if there were more of them or if they could be encouraged to breed. She shared this last thought with Mass-mind, but something was lost in the excitement, and the thought that filtered through was reduced to "Large Crawlers Spotted. New Food Source." As soon as the crawlers—first one, then the other—ventured far enough onto the Mass surface, Mass-mind had attempted to absorb them.

***

The Gismo sat on Pauli's bunk where Dennison had dropped it. Pauli noticed a small red light flashing on the console.

"Why's the Gismo flashing?" he said.

Dennison picked it up and read the display. The lake was stuffed with rare minerals: Magmanite, Petrazine, Avaltium. Resetting the instrument, he said, "It's a false reading. I expect it was damaged when you dropped it."

"This life-form," said Pauli. "Do you think it might be intelligent?"

"That's a bit of a leap, Crewman."

***

eVVe had an amazing thought. She suggested it to her mother first, and the Empress dismissed the idea; it was just the sort of crazy notion that she had grown to expect from her delinquent daughter. eVVe took her amazing notion to oAAo, the great philosopher.

oAAo thought about it. The idea was outlandish, bordering on insanity. And yet... Could these crawlers be intelligent, sentient beings?

The new crawlers were unlike any of the native ~mmmmmmg species. These were much bigger. They had only four legs, although they used only two to move about on. It was difficult to understand how they managed to stay upright. Could this balancing feat be indicative of intelligence? The native crawlers reflected very little light, but these new specimens were almost as bright as S1, and they had no tails. Their movements had been unusual. They had left the safety of the rock and moved across the Mass surface, apparently without fear. And then they had defended themselves against absorption. The way they had arrived in that split boulder – that was the most convincing piece of evidence. Had they hollowed out the crevice in that boulder? If they had, they might indeed be intelligent.

***

Dennison thought about what his crewman had said. Could the lake be sentient? The way it rippled and the way it lay on the side of that mountain were not natural. Then there was its reaction to Pauli's blade, possibly the strongest indicator. And what about the way they had fallen into the lake? It was as if the lake sucked them down and then spat them out. Were those instinctive reactions? Dennison didn't think so. But did all of this add up to a conscious, intelligent mind? Dennison wasn't sure. He decided to conduct a simple test.

"I don't like it, Skipper."

"Nothing to worry about. I should be back in ten minutes, fifteen, tops."

"I still don't like it."

"Don't be a worrywart. Zip me up and hand me those Go stones."

Captain Dennison made his way down to the yellow lake. A recent downpour had left a cloud of heavy mist shimmering in the unnatural light and clinging to the surface of the lake as far as the eye could see.

The captain fished a handful of white Go stones from the bag and laid them in a heap on a flat piece of ground close to the lake shore. Then he turned on his heels and hurried back to the shuttle.

***

On the Galactic Explorer preparations were under way for a full-scale ground-fall mission. One shuttle would drop the five-man geological survey team; the other two would carry a company of armed Marines. You couldn't be too careful on unexplored planets. The countdown had started: Departure would commence noon the following day (to avoid confusion, the GE Millington kept Earth time through its away missions). All that remained was for Captain Dennison to make his report to the Commander.

"Report!" the Commander roared into the radio handset. Dennison could tell from the Commander's voice that he was chewing on one of his famous cigars.

"We found creeper-crawlies, Commander. Big ones."

"What about the mineral deposits?"

"No sign of those, sir." Dennison was astounded at his own lie. He had no foreknowledge of his intention to deceive. He looked at Pauli, whose eyebrows were doing the quickstep.

"That's disappointing. Any vegetation?"

"No vegetation, sir."

"Was there anything else?"

Dennison hesitated. "There's something weird down here, sir."

"What kind of something?"

"I'm not sure, sir, but I'm pretty sure it was a lifeform."

"Another bug?"

"Not a bug, sir. This was much bigger."

"What did it look like?"

"Yellow. And flat, like a big lake."

"How big?"

"Lake Superior big."

"*That* big." The Commander paused for thought. The radio hissed. "You took a sample?"

"No, sir. We tried, but it backed off."

"Backed? Off?"

"Yes, sir. It saw Pauli's knife and backed off."

"You're sure you weren't hallucinating? Have you checked your air supply?"

"I'm sure, sir."

"Well try again, man, and try harder next time. Get me a sample."

"I left some stones by the lake."

"Stones?"

"Yes, sir. White Go stones."

"Your point being?"

"I'm hoping the lifeform might..."

"Might what? Suggest a game of Go?"

"I'm hoping it might do something with the stones."

"Like what?"

"Something intelligent, sir."

***

They waited two hours. In that time it rained five times. Pauli counted.

Captain Dennison broke out the spare spacesuit and they made their way back to the shore of the lake. The readout on Pauli's headset showed a temperature increase of five degrees. The red giant's brooding presence filled the sky; the smaller sun was nowhere to be seen.

The white stones had been rearranged into a line in small groups: one stone, then two, three, five, seven, eleven, thirteen.

"Those are the primes," Pauli said, his voice hushed.

"You know what this means, Pauli?" Dennison peered at his crewman through his visor.

"We're outnumbered, Skipper?"

"Damn right. Let's take our sample and get back to the shuttle."

Captain Dennison stood by with the Gismo while his crewman stepped onto the lake, blade in one hand, a small sample container in the other.

Pauli hunkered down and deftly sliced a small square of material from the surface of the lake. The lake rippled. It heaved with undulations like a sea of molasses inhabited by a million whales. Pauli lost his balance and dropped the sample.

The moment the sample hit the surface, it vanished.

"Where'd it go?"

"Never mind, Crewman. Take another sample and let's get out of here."

Pauli placed one knee on the surface, and sliced off a second sample. Again, the surface of the lake reacted as before, but this time Pauli managed to get the sample into the container and close the lid.

Before he could regain his feet, a tentacle of yellow material zipped out and locked around the top joint of the crewman's index finger.

Pauli screamed. "Holy *crap*! It's got hold of my finger!"

He tried to pull himself free, but the harder he tugged, the tighter the tentacle squeezed. Then a second tentacle sprouted from the first and wrapped itself around Pauli's hand.

"Use your knife," Dennison shouted.

Pauli slashed out at the tentacles and cut himself free.

"Run for it, Crewman!" Dennison shouted.

Back in their shuttle Dennison gave his crewman a shot of medicinal Bourbon to calm his nerves.

Pauli's hand was red, his finger swollen. He downed the liquor in one slug. "They didn't teach us about that in training," he said.

"I think they did," Dennison replied.

"I musta missed that class."

"That was an intelligent lifeform, Pauli. Nothing like anything we've seen before, I grant you, but an intelligence just the same."

"And it grabbed for my hand why?"

"I expect it was protecting itself. Yours was the first hostile act."

Pauli's finger was throbbing. He said, "It had a grip like a vice. I can still feel where it held the end of my finger."

"It's bound to be sore for awhile," Dennison said. "You'll have to put some ice on it when we get back to the ship. I could give you a morphine shot now, if you like."

"No thanks, Skipper, but I could use another shot of Bourbon."

Dennison poured his crewman another finger of Bourbon. Pauli wrapped his good hand around the glass and stared through the window at the desolate scene outside. The rain had started again.

***

eVVe watched as the shiny crawlers scuttled back to the crevice in their boulder. Then she saw fire emerge from the bottom of the shiny boulder as it rose slowly from its perch. Now she was convinced. Who had ever seen a boulder do anything like that? The boulder gathered speed and disappeared into the murky sky.

***

"Well, did you get me a sample?" The Commander was chewing on one of his famous cigars.

"Yes, sir,"

"What about your experiment with the Go stones?"

"That was a success, Commander. I left the stones in a small heap and when I returned the lake had arranged them in a recognizable sequence."

"So you believe this lake is sentient?"

"Beyond question."

"Intelligent?"

"No doubt about it, sir."

There was a long pause. The commander puffed on his cigar, filling the cabin with acrid smoke. The expression on his face turned sour.

"Your recommendation, Captain?"

"We should attempt to communicate with it, Commander."

"And how would you suggest we do that?"

Another long pause. The commander continued sucking the life from his cigar.

Dennison said, "Perhaps we should take a rain check on this planet, sir."

"And ignore the spectrometric readings, the minerals?"

"The planet's environment is too hostile for practical purposes, sir. There are active volcanoes everywhere and frequent earthquakes, and the atmosphere is poisonous."

"So you think we should forget about it and move on."

"Yes, sir."

The commander ground his cigar out in a large ashtray. "Get the sample to the lab and let's see what the professor makes of it."

***

Ripples ran in every direction over the surface of the lake as the argument raged. Mass–mind was convinced that these new crawlers were a very promising food source. The crawlers must be captured. It would be foolish to ignore this S1-given opportunity to detain a breeding pair.

A minority amongst the Mass, headed by oAAo was convinced that these crawlers were intelligent visitors from another world. They should not be harmed. Mass-mind had a responsibility to try to communicate with them, not to eat them. The majority disagreed. How could crawlers be intelligent? The idea was preposterous!

***

Professor Velikof Zonk VI was finding it hard to think straight. One of the fleet's most experienced exobiologists, with twenty years of deep space travel under his belt, he had never seen anything like this. The sample under the lens of his microscope was bizarre. It was more than that. It was so grotesque, so mind-bogglingly weird that the professor struggled for adjectives to describe it. What he was looking at was a lifeform as alien as anything that he had ever come across, something totally beyond-Darwinian. He knew that a Nobel Prize was a slam dunk if he could get anybody in the scientific world on Earth to believe him. He had to remind himself to breathe.

"Well, Professor?" Captain Dennison was becoming impatient.

Professor Zonk replied without looking up from his microscope, "You say there's a lake of this, ah, material down there?

"A large lake, yes."

"Amazing! Utterly astounding! A large lake, you say."

"But can you say what it is, Professor?"

Zonk waved a hand at the captain. "Not yet," he said. "I need time to study it, time to carry out zome tests."

"Can't you tell me anything?"

The Professor sighed and sat back in his chair.

"It's a lifeform," he said, "no question aboudit. A thin membranous creature with an elastic, porous epicuticle—"

"Epi—?"

"Epicuticle. A thin waxy waterproof skin, like a frog's. I believe some of the pores may be eye holes, like rows and rows of pinhole cameras. You remember the Box Brownie, Kapitan?" Dennison grunted. "Well, here we haff rows and rows of Box Brownies, providing the creature with a myriad monochromatic images of the world around it."

"How many?"

"How many eyes, you mean?"

"Yes."

"That is difficult to estimate. This zample alone contains one thousand pinhole pores, approggzimately. We must allow for the possibility that some of these pores may be used for other functions, such as eating and drinking and breathing—if the creature breathes, which is by no means certain—and eggcretion, but even so, the creature's vision must be remarkable."

Dennison gasped. "One thousand pores in a four-by-three inch sample!"

The professor nodded, his glasses sliding to the end of his nose. "Yes, indeed. The rate of porosity is aztronomically high, say one hundred thousand per square meter, and yet the creature's skin is entirely waterproof."

"How is that possible?"

"Remember your high school physics, Kapitan. Zurface tension effectively limits the size of a water drop. Below a certain size water will not easily penetrate the pores."

"That is pretty amazing," said Dennison.

"This is nothing. Consider that what we haff here is one complete entity—"

"But my crewman cut a piece—"

"Even so, this is one entire entity, not a part of one, but a whole, complete being. I could take a knife and split it into two parts and I would have two entities, complete in every way."

"Two smaller entities?"

"Smaller, *ja*, but complete nonetheless. You will observe that the creature is uniform in every direction. North equals south, south equals east, east and west are indistinguishable. Hmm?"

"Yes, I can see that."

"From this we can deduce that the creature is a female. Having no chenitalia, it reproduces asexually. Have you heard of the bdelloid rotifers?"

"No, I don't think so."

"The bdelloid rotifers are the only creatures on Earth that are known to reproduce asexually, and its kind has no males."

"You mean that these creatures are all females?"

"Certainly. What is more, I would hazard a guess that they reproduce by whole body mitosis."

"Like cell division?"

"Indeed. They expand and grow in two dimensions, and when they reach a certain size, they split. Zimple."

"And is that how the belloid—?"

"Is that how the bdelloid rotifers reproduce? No. Nothing on Earth reproduces like these creatures."

"And have you detected intelligence, Professor?"

"Oh yes, beyond question."

"So the creature has a brain, a nervous system?"

Professor Zonk shook his bald head. "No. No nervous system. And no brain as we might imagine it."

"How can it think without a brain?"

"That question will require eggsensive study, Kapitan, but it seems to me that the entire creature may be made up of tissue capable of propagating thought."

Dennison took a few moments to absorb this revelation. Then he said, "May I?" nodding toward the microscope.

"Please."

Under the microscope Dennison could see the pin holes. They didn't look like eyes—or cameras—and yet the captain had the eerie feeling that he was being watched.

***

Once again eVVe saw the shiny boulders descend from the clouds. Three of them, this time, appeared in the dusky sky, floated down and settled on a nearby flat, rocky surface. An unimaginably large number of pinhole eyes turned to watch as the three boulders opened and disgorged their cargo of large crawlers. eVVe counted them as they emerged. She lost count at twenty-five.

***

In recognition of his specialist knowledge of the planet, Captain Dennison was given overall command of the ground-fall mission. He briefed the whole team, warning them not to venture on to the lake under any circumstances. Once the Marines were deployed along the shore of the lake, the geological team took up their positions. At a signal from the captain, the survey began. Armed with their Gismos, the geophysicists began a systematic survey of the edge of the lake and the surrounding landscape. Dennison took up a position to the rear of the line of Marines, where he could keep an eye on the whole team.

The silence of the mission's communications net was punctuated by whoops of glee and laughter as the first mineral deposits were discovered, but then, as these discoveries became commonplace, silence returned to the airwaves.

The survey took close to two hours. It was only when the time came to return to their shuttles that Dennison realized the lake had shifted. Circling around behind them, it now surrounded them on all sides, and a wide, static yellow river stood between them and their shuttles.

Their retreat had been cut off. The only way back to the shuttles was across the lake. Dennison sent a message to the Galactic Explorer, and gave the order.

"We're going to have to cross the lake, men. Set your Gismos to electrolytic charge and run for your lives."

The team made a dash toward the shuttles.

Once all the team members were on the lake, it began to suck them in. One by one their boots sank into the ooze.

Many of the Marines emptied their weapons into the lake, to no avail.

"Use your Gismos!" Dennison shouted.

And they did. On all sides the geophysicists zapped the lake with sparks from their Gismos. But the electrolytic discharges had no effect; the men continued to sink.

"It's not working, Captain!" one of the scientists cried.

"I can see that," Dennison snapped. "The life-form has adapted."

"What else can we try?"

Dennison made no reply. He had no reply to make.

***

"What happened?" the Commander asked.

"I'm not sure, sir. I guess we just got propitious."

"Lucky. You mean you got lucky?"

"Lucky, yes, sir. We were sinking fast. The Gismos were useless as a defense. Some of the men had disappeared below the surface. And just when I thought we were all going to die, the lake ejected us."

"All of you? Just like that?"

"Yes, sir. I couldn't believe it."

"Right, I'm going report this system as non-productive. We'll move on. Maybe we'll have more luck someplace else."

***

It had fallen to the Empress to decide whether to communicate with the crawlers or eat them, and she had decided that Mass should accept the munificence bestowed on it by the Gods; the large crawlers would be absorbed. She informed Mass-mind of her decision, then slithered away on her own to do some thinking.

When the Empress returned, she discovered that the Mass had let the crawlers go. She was livid. She demanded to know what happened.

eVVe explained.

As soon as all of the crawlers were on the surface of the planet, Mass began to move. Slowly, slowly, Mass slithered around behind them, until the crawlers were surrounded. There could be no escape. When they had no other way out, the crawlers made a dash across the Mass toward the safety of their boulders, as Mass-mind knew they would, and they were sucked down into the Mass's ooze. The process of absorption began.

The Empress said, "But the crawlers were not absorbed."

"No, mother, they were not absorbed.

"So what went wrong? Did they use their flashing rocks again? Was that it?"

"It is true that the crawlers tried to free themselves using their flashing rocks," eVVe replied, "but Mass was prepared for that. The flashing rocks were neutralized."

"So what happened? Why did we let them go?"

"The crawlers could not be absorbed."

"Could not? Why not?"

"Mass made every effort to absorb them."

"Without success."

"Without success."

"So what was the problem?"
eVVe said, "Absorption proved impossible."
"Yes, but why?"
"It's simple, mother. We couldn't get the wrapping off."

THE PERFECT WOMAN

HE SWUNG THE LABORATORY doors closed. The doors were massive, three inches thick and ten feet high, made of ancient oak from the Black Forest and reinforced with metal studs. He thought: Thank God for the warlords of the twelfth century.

"And the Third Reich," he said aloud, as he slid home the huge cast-iron bolt.

The crash of the doors and the clang of the bolt echoed around him and faded to silence. He stood perfectly still for a while, chasing the memory of the sounds from his mind, re-tuning his hearing to the absolute silence .

He waited until the only sound he could hear was his own breathing and his eyes had adjusted to the gloom. Then he moved away from the door and started up the stone staircase. Following the inner curve of the castle wall, the stairs passed under a tall stained-glass window. A shaft of moonlight glinted on his bald head, catching his gaunt features, his hooked nose, his ugly mouth, scarred and twisted in pain. He was near-naked, his bleached skin hanging in folds, barely covering his angular bones. He stumbled, leaving a bloody handprint on the wall, and then rested on the cold stone step under the disinterested gaze of a long-forgotten ancestor, frozen in victorious pose over a slain enemy.

From behind the laboratory doors, from the bowels of the great castle below, faint sounds emerged. The growl of an animal? No. Ghastly as the sounds were, they were human: an anguished groan, a muffled blood-curdling howl, followed by a ghastly sound like a strangled scream.

"God preserve me," he whispered.

Picking himself up, he pressed on to the first landing and into the library, closing and locking the door behind him. He slipped into a dressing gown and lowered his misshapen body into a chair.

He lit a lamp and propped it up on the desk in front of him. Painfully, he slipped the dressing gown off his shoulders revealing a deep, gaping wound in his side. His clothes lay over the back of the chair. He tore his shirt into strips, and improvised a bandage to dress the wound. He paused to rest briefly, then, with trembling fingers, pulled out some paper, scattering several blood-spattered sheets on the floor, dipped his pen in the inkwell and began to write.

I am dying. This is my last testament—the last record of my life's work. I write it in the hope that it will be read and acted upon by whosoever finds my body, for the future of mankind surely depends on it.

The ramblings of a deranged mind, you may think. No, my friend, not so. Keep your mind open and read on. If I live long enough to complete this account, all will become clear.

I am a scientist. When you read what I have done you will understand how the result of my work threatens the future of civilization, and even the very future of the human race. A mad scientist, then, you say. No, not mad. Misguided, perhaps. Well-intentioned, certainly. And I freely admit with the benefit of hindsight that I should never have started this accursed project.

My name is unimportant. My field is Medicine—of a sort—Medical Anthropology, I call it.

Blood from his damaged lip dropped on the paper. He brushed it away with a grunt of impatience, and continued writing.

My reputation in the field of human anatomy is well-established—and well known. I studied under the patronage of the late Baron von Frankenstein, my tutor and mentor, and was employed as his assistant for many years. The baron dedicated himself to his dream of recreating the miracle of life in the laboratory. His work was based on an unshakeable conviction that death was not simply the end of life, but merely a temporary interruption to life's flow. He and I spent months debating this concept, which I now fully share.

But noble as his aims were, the Baron's methods were crude and often ill-conceived. Driven by personal ambition, he was impatient for tangible results. He sacrificed all caution and scientific precision in his haste to reach his ultimate goal, without a care for the quality of the end product.

Even so, his achievements were immense and when the hysteria of the modern age has abated, I have no doubt that history will laud his immense contribution to medical science.

The old man paused and strained to listen. He heard nothing but the hiss and splutter of the lamp flame. He turned the flame down and listened again. Then he heard it. A faint scratching, scrabbling sound and a muffled whimper, followed by three dull thuds from behind the laboratory door. Please God make it hold! He shuddered, turned up the flame and resumed his chronicle.

After the Baron's sudden and tragic death, I resolved to continue his work, but taking meticulous care and using the full scientific method. Check, double-check and counter-check were applied stringently to verify every small step of the process, and to ensure that every advance could be produced and reproduced at will. Nothing was left to chance. My work progressed slowly. Several years passed. Years of painstaking work, when my form was not seen by any mortal man save my two faithful grave-diggers who kept me supplied with bodies, from which I drew spare parts for my experiments.

At last, I reached the point where I was certain that I could reproduce the work of the Baron—I could bring life to a cadaver, replacing any defective or injured internal or external organ. My surgical skills were supreme and had advanced well beyond von Frankenstein's crudities. My subjects, even the ones made up of multiple transplants, showed no outward signs of my work. They carried no ugly sutures, bore no visible scars and were outwardly indistinguishable from any man—or woman—naturally born.

Yes, they were perfect in every detail, warm to the touch, with hair that grew and blood that coursed through their veins. Outwardly perfect in every detail.

When it came to the workings of the brain, however, I ran into a major obstacle. I had no difficulty instilling life into the organ. Even those that had been dead for several days responded well to electroinfusion therapy. I could produce alpha and beta brain activity at will. Responses to external stimuli were obtained and catalogued. I even recorded evidence of REM sleep in some subjects. It is all there in my records. Everything was just as it should have been. My subjects were alive, awake, conscious and mobile. By any established scientific measurement, they should have been complete human beings, each ready to take his or her place in the world. But, they were all quite mad. Every one of them—deranged beyond retrieval.

A further year of research identified the problem. It seems that, at the moment of death, a small ganglial connection between upper and lower brain is destroyed. This ganglion carries millions of synaptic nerves, consisting of hundreds of millions of neurons, which carry information between the upper and lower brain, suppressing lower animal-in-stinctual responses and enabling higher cognitive reasoning functions to predominate.

Immediately, I set about perfecting the microsurgical pro-cedures necessary to activate the ganglial connection. A year passed. Then two more. My microsurgical skills multiplied tenfold, surpassing the skills of even the most eminent Harley Street surgeon, but still the vital procedure eluded me. My two faithful grave-diggers kept me supplied with corpses in ever greater quantities, settling in to a sort of macabre rhythm, each night delivering two fresh subjects and taking away for disposal the remains of those delivered the night before.

There was a loud dull thump from below, followed by another. He opened the door a crack and peered out. Darkness was falling outside, and there was very little light coming in through the window. He could see nothing. He stepped out, and started down the stone steps. There was a crash from behind the laboratory door. Then an-other crash and another and another and another. As the crashing continued, ever louder, faster, more insistent, he hurried back to his desk in the library. He resumed his seat, dipped his pen in the ink, and wrote with trembling hand.

Eventually, it began to dawn on me that what I was attempting may be impossible. Much as the notion would have been alien to Baron von Frankenstein, and much as I was desperate to reject it, I began to think that perhaps, after all, there may be some corporeal transformations brought about by death which are irreversible.

Once the seed of doubt was planted in my mind, it began to grow, intruding on my thoughts and disturbing my concentration. My work began to suffer. I struggled on, making stupid mistakes and wasting several subjects. Then, in a rage, I smashed half the glass equipment in the laboratory, frightening the grave-diggers away from the castle, before retiring to my library with a bottle of brandy.

I drank myself into a stupor.

That night I slept at my desk. I slept long and peacefully, probably for the first time in years, and when I awoke, I had the answer.

The key to the problem lay in my approach. In every respect, and for every major organ, every artery, every limb, my approach had always been one of repair, renewal and revitalization—using existing organs and tissue from the subject or transplanted from others. Now I knew where the answer lay—I would build the ganglion connection from scratch, using inorganic materials.

A radical approach, you may think. And I would agree with you, but after so many unsuccessful attempts, so many sleepless nights, so many failures, I knew that this was what I had to do, although I lacked the technical knowledge and the skills to complete the task.

He coughed and there was the taste of blood in his mouth. It was as he feared—his lung had been punctured by the knife. His time was running out. He checked his crude bandages and found them saturated, but the flow from the wound had been staunched. He wrote on.

The next six months I devoted to the written works of Benjamin Franklin, of Faraday and the young Maxwell. Thus I assimilated the new sciences of electricity and magnetism and began to search for a solution to my problem. Using repeated trial and error, it took no more than nine further months to build a device which enabled primitive communication between the two brain structures. From there, the device was modified and refined, extended, and miniaturized until I had perfected it.

He put his pen down and moved to the door, opening it a crack. The crashing sounds were now less frequent, perhaps fifteen seconds apart, but each one impacted the door with terrifying force. Heart thumping wildly, he tried to imagine what object or implement could be used to produce such pounding. Then, mixed in with the crashing he thought he heard the sound of splintering wood and his blood froze. He scurried back to his desk.

On Christmas day last year, the grave-diggers brought me in a fresh corpse. It was the body of a young woman of twenty-two or twenty-three years, tragically killed under the wheels of a runaway carriage. I set to work. Her spleen was ruptured and her liver had been damaged, though not severely. The spleen I replaced immediately; the damaged tissue I removed from her liver. The rest of her organs were in fine condition.. Her thighs were a little over-full and her breasts a little small to my eye, so I took a couple of hours to correct these minor blemishes. Once I was happy with her anatomy and pleased with her outward appearance, I reconnected her mid-brain ganglion using my non-organic device.

The whole procedure took less than twelve hours, at the end of which time I plugged her in to the electroinfusion apparatus. The revitalizing procedure went without a hitch, and as the blood transfusions neared completion, I gazed with awe at the beautiful creature before me. Slowly, her body temperature returned to normal and her skin color lost the pallor of death. Her breathing seemed easy and natural, her ECG readings looked promising and all of her reflexes tested normal. She lay on the slab, sleeping soundly, like the beautiful sleeping princess of the fairytale. I decided to call her "Princess" as a convenient working name.

She slept for four hours. When she awoke, she opened her eyes and looked up at me and I could tell instantly that I had succeeded. The look in her eyes was calm and thoughtful, with not a sign of dementia. Here, at last was the final culmination of my work, the final vindication of my methods and absolutely incontrovertible proof that the Baron's theories were sound.

I had created the perfect woman.

The extensive tests that followed proved that her mind was indeed intact and functioning perfectly. All of her memories had been erased, but her capacity to learn was totally unaffected. I began to teach her. I taught her how to walk, to cook, to clean and to sew. And I taught her to talk. This was the one area where her progress was slow. She quickly mastered a basic vocabulary of perhaps two hundred words, but she had no real concept of sentence construction. She could communicate quite well, using phrases like "Princess food cook" and "Master book show Princess"—she called me "Master".

Within three months, she was fulfilling all of the functions of a dutiful housewife. I discovered that she had a fine, intelligent mind, so I introduced her to the work of the Renaissance masters, Leonardo da Vinci, Michelangelo, Raphael and Donatello.

She seemed happy. I certainly was. Here was my life's work, walking and talking, breathing, enjoying the works of the great artists; under my tutelage her culinary skills progressed in leaps and bounds. I could feel myself falling in love with her. And she with me? Perhaps. Perhaps not. Is it love, when a chick emerges from its shell and forms an attachment to the hen? Or when a barnacle attaches itself to the back of a whale? For she was dependent on me as is the chick to the hen or the barnacle to the whale.

He put his pen down and went to the door again. He could hear nothing. He stepped out into the passageway. A wave of dizziness washed over him. He was very weak; he had lost a lot of blood. He steadied himself, and moved cautiously down the steps to the laboratory door. Silence. Absolute silence. He put his ear to the door, but still he could hear nothing. He tested the door and the iron bolt. They seemed secure, although there was some detectable movement of the door in its jamb. He turned, made his way slowly back up the steps to the library, and resumed his seat.

I fell hopelessly in love with my creation. And now I was faced with a serious dilemma, for my Princess was as innocent as a babe in arms. A fully grown and fully formed woman she was; fully familiar with the paintings and sculp-

tures of the Masters, but of matters of the heart or of the temptations of the flesh she had no inkling.

I tried to teach her the basics of human anatomy and the principles of the reproductive process, but it was hopeless. Her vocabulary was so limited, and her lack of understanding of basic biology such an insurmountable stumbling-block. It was like trying to explain the steam engine to a five-year-old; she had absolutely no idea what I was talking about. I tried kissing her, but she must have thought this a novel way of eating, for she bit a piece from my lower lip.

Finally, today, I decided that I would have to show her what I could not explain to her in words. I waited until after we had finished a meal, and then I took off my clothes and stood before her. "Man" I said. "Man". She took one look at my naked body, and burst into laughter. She jumped up and ran to the library, returning with a picture of Michelangelo's David. She held the picture up for me to see and, still laughing, she shook her head and said "Man," pointing at the picture.

I held her in my arms, but she struggled free and ran away into the kitchen. I followed her. I found her huddled in a corner of the room, still clutching the book and repeating "man, man" over and over to herself. I went over to her. She stood up and came towards me, a sharp unaccustomed glint in her eye. Too late, I saw the knife in her hand.

At that moment, the castle was rocked by a huge explosion.

"Merciful God!" he said.

He dropped his pen and staggered over to the library door. Outside, the passageway was full of dust and smoke. He descended a few steps. The laboratory doors had been blown off its hinges. Princess was nowhere to be seen.

He turned and hurried back to the library. Closing and locking the door behind him, he picked up his pen and continued his chronicle:

The end is near. I am weak from loss of blood and my Princess has escaped from the laboratory. The only question that remains is whether she will break in here and finish me off before I die from my wound.

I suppose I should not be surprised at what happened. After all, what other reaction could one expect from the perfect woman when confronted by the imperfect figure of the average man? To whomever finds this manuscript, I urge you destroy all of my records. What I have accomplished must never be repeated. The world as we know it would never be safe for men if

There was a sound behind him. He turned. The last thing he saw was the flash of lamplight on naked steel.

ACKNOWLEDGMENTS

This book would not have been possible without the invaluable assistance of my editor, Nora Pelizzari and cover designer, Rachel Lawston. Research for EGGS was by Vicki Tieche.

Dean Wesley Smith and Kristine Kathryn Rusch must take some of the blame for scaring me away from literary agents, literary contracts, and traditional publishers.

My brother, Dave, sister, Judy, and daughter, Roisin, helped as beta readers. My two sons, Brian and David provided inspiration and ideas.

My ever-suffering wife must take most of the acolytes for reading my stuff in its rawest form and for putting up with my obsessive behavior and poor spelling. As soon as this book is published I will tackle all those jobs around the house that I have neglected over the past 15 years. I promise.

ABOUT JJ TONER

I AM A FULL-TIME writer. I write short stories and novels. When not sitting at my computer writing or surfing the net, you'll find me reading or watching golf on TV. In earlier lives I was an oil worker, an engineer, a computer programmer, a factory worker, a teacher, a computer manager, a support worker, a smoker and a drinker. I even took exercise once upon a time. I live in Ireland with my wife and youngest son.

JJToner.com

BOOKS BY JJ TONER

HOUDINI'S HANDCUFFS, A NOIR Detective Thriller, featuring DI Ben Jordan

Find Emily, a second DI Jordan Detective Thriller
Retribution and Other Stories, Crime Shorts

The Black Orchestra, a WW2 spy thriller
The Wings of the Eagle, the second WW2 Spy Thriller in the Black Orchestra series
A Postcard from Hamburg, the third WW2 Spy Thriller in the series
The Gingerbread Spy, the fourth WW2 Spy Thriller in the series
The Serpent's Egg, Red Orchestra WW2 Spy Thriller
Liberaton Berlin, a WW2 novel

Zugzwang, a pre-war detective story featuring Kommissar Saxon
Queen Sacrifice, a second case for Kommissar Saxon
The White Knight, a third case for Kommissar Saxon

EGGS and Other Stories, a collection of fun SF short stories
The Shape of Fear – Android Wars book 1

Escape from Luciflex – Android Wars book 2